"I'm sick of kisses that taste of drink."

Zane paused, and Deborah winced at his implied reference to his wife.

Suddenly his fingers were curling into the sleek bun at the back of Deborah's neck, destroying its tidiness. He held her head still, as if he expected resistance. Then his mouth descended to her lips. He devoured them hungrily, savoring and exploring, plundering their softness.

Deborah felt her desire rising to the fever pitch of his. Common sense screamed its alarm, warning her of the danger of his seduction.

Her mind fought through the heady sensations to remind her: after the joy would come bitterness. Deborah realized this might be her only chance to stop this scene from reaching its climax—from ruining them both. She could stop it now... if she wanted to.

JANET DAILEY AMERICANA

Every novel in this collection is your passport
to a romantic tour of the United States through
time-honored favorites by America's First Lady
of romance fiction. Each of the fifty novels is
set in a different state, researched by Janet and
her husband, Bill. For the Daileys it was an
odyssey of discovery. For you, it's the journey
of a lifetime.

Janet Dailey Americana

ALABAMA—Dangerous Masquerade
ALASKA—Northern Magic
ARIZONA—Sonora Sundown
ARKANSAS—Valley of the Vapours
CALIFORNIA—Fire and Ice
COLORADO—After the Storm
CONNECTICUT—Difficult Decision
DELAWARE—The Matchmakers

These books may be available at your local bookseller.

Don't miss any of our special offers. Write to us at the
following address for information on our newest releases.

Harlequin Reader Service
901 Fuhrmann Blvd., P.O. Box 1397, Buffalo, NY 14240
Canadian address: P.O. Box 609,
Fort Erie, Ont. L2A 9Z9

Janet Dailey
Americana

DIFFICULT DECISION

Harlequin Books

TORONTO • NEW YORK • LONDON
AMSTERDAM • PARIS • SYDNEY • HAMBURG
STOCKHOLM • ATHENS • TOKYO • MILAN

The state flower depicted on the cover is mountain laurel.

Janet Dailey Americana edition published September 1986
ISBN 373-89807-X

Harlequin Presents edition published October 1980
Second printing October 1982

Original hardcover edition published in 1980
by Mills & Boon Limited

CHAPTER ONE

THE DOOR TO THE INNER OFFICE swung open and another job applicant walked out. The look on the man's face said he didn't know how the interview had turned out, but there was relief on his resigned expression. Deborah Holland felt all her muscles tensing as the secretary gave the man a cool smile of dismissal and glanced at the next name on her list. There were three applicants sitting in the outer office, including Deborah. The names had not been called in the order of their arrival so she had no idea who would be interviewed next.

The intercom buzzed, a signal that the next applicant was to be sent in. The woman looked up, smiling that distant smile of hers. "Ms. Drummond, you may go in now."

Deborah's stomach knotted even tighter as the woman on the sofa next to her rose to walk across the room to the solid oak door. She studied her competition, gray eyes sweeping the efficient-looking woman in her mid-forties. It was impossible to be objective. Concealing a sigh, Deborah reached in the outer pocket of her purse for the pack of cigarettes and her lighter. The spectacled man in the chair next to the sofa leaned forward to offer her a light, but the flame of her lighter was already curling around the tip of her cigarette.

"An evil habit," she said and blew out a thin stream of smoke. Her thumbnail nervously ran over the filtered end of the cigarette, her only outward display of strain.

"Yes," he agreed with her statement and lighted a cigarette of his own. "But it's a great tranquilizer for the nerves when you're waiting. My name is Bob Campbell."

Veiling her assessing look behind auburn-tipped lashes, she considered his gesture of friendliness to be quite pointless. In his late thirties, the man appeared highly qualified for the position. His quietly strong features gave the impression that he was both dependable and experienced. No matter who got the job, there would be no occasion for them to meet again. Deborah had never indulged in idle flirtation, and after twenty-six years she found no reason to begin now.

"How do you do," she nodded politely, but didn't introduce herself. She intended to do everything she could to beat him out of this job. It seemed hypocritical to respond to his friendly overtures, even if his only intention was to pass the time.

The secretary behind the desk began typing. The next couple of minutes were dominated by the racing keys of the typewriter tapping across the paper. Deborah leaned forward to flick the ash from her cigarette into the chrome ashtray. There was a natural, fluid grace to her movement.

"This will be my third interview," Bob Campbell volunteered the information. "How about you?"

"Yes." Her hand automatically inched the hem of her royal blue skirt down to cover her shapely knees.

"They have screened a lot of applicants for this job. I guess we should consider ourselves honored we're still in the running now that the field has been narrowed down to five."

"That doesn't pay the rent." Deborah ground the butt of her cigarette in the ashtray. As far as she was concerned, her attitude was realistic. If others, including Bob Campbell, considered it to be hard, they were entitled to their opinion. It meant nothing to her. Being one of five was not a consolation unless she was the one who obtained the job.

"True," he admitted and eyed her through the thick lenses of his glasses. The opening of the connecting door distracted him from his study of her. The woman who had entered the private office only minutes before exited the room without so much as a glance at the other occupants.

"That was quick," Bob Campbell murmured sotto voce to Deborah. "It looks like the field is down to four."

Deborah cast a speculative glance at the departing applicant and silently agreed with his conclusion. The buzz of the intercom tautened her nerves, stringing them out on tenterhooks.

"You may go in, Miss Holland," the secretary instructed and resumed her typing.

Her heart skipped several beats in a row, but this inner vulnerability was well armored with her iron poise. Straightening from the sofa with apparent calm, Deborah ignored the nervous convulsions in her stomach. Job interviews were always confidence-destroying experiences, but she would not reveal that she was equally susceptible to the malady.

"Good luck," her competition wished her and Deborah thought it was a foolish thing for him to do.

Entering the private office, Deborah closed the door quietly behind her. Her footsteps made no sound on the plushly thick carpeting in autumn shades as she walked to the oak desk. The man seated behind it was studying her résumé. He didn't look up when she approached, but she didn't doubt for a minute that he was aware of her presence.

Silently she waited for him to acknowledge her, taking the opportunity to study her possible prospective employer. When she had been called back after the first interview, Deborah had attempted to find out more about the man she would be working for. She had garnered little information beyond his name and vital statistics: Z. Wilding, born thirty-eight years ago, married, no children. Since he had assumed control of LaCosta Enterprises twelve years ago, the firm had grown virtually into a conglomerate, which said something for the aggressiveness and ability of the man who ran it. But Deborah hadn't been able to learn much beyond that. He stayed well in the background, an invisible power pulling the strings.

Yet the broad-shouldered man before her would never be regarded as a nonentity. Deborah found herself wondering how he had managed to remain behind the scenes. What she could glimpse of his craggy male features and the suggestion of height in his muscular build indicated a compelling masculinity. The luster of his jet black hair was subdued by its unruly tendencies. Its darkness coupled with the sun-bronzed complexion of his skin added to his attraction. His looks alone would command attention; his influential position would demand it. So why was she able to find out so little about him from the newspaper files and the various consumer institutions?

With the indolent ease of one accustomed to people waiting on him, he lifted his head to look at her. Deborah found herself gazing into a pair of shattering blue eyes and a face that seemed almost literally chiseled in bronze. The features were relentlessly hard and cynical, flagrantly male and ruthless. His dark, ice-blue eyes were emotionless in their inspection of her. From her memory bank, Deborah recalled a college lecture that had expounded the theory that blue-eyed people tended to be more calculating and less influenced by emotion, capable of putting aside their own personal feelings to regard a given situation abstractly. Supposedly a predominant number of race-car drivers, astronauts and pilots were blue eyed, and better qualified because of this so-called inherent ability for detached analysis.

Detached, emotionless, calculating—these adjectives aptly described the man who was now assessing her. His indifferent blue gaze noted the dark auburn color of her hair smoothed back in a businesslike coil at the nape of her neck, swept disinterestedly over the shapely curves of her figure beneath the classic simplicity of her suit, and returned to peruse the résumé in his hand.

Not once was there a flicker of male admiration for her obvious beauty, and Deborah hadn't reached the age of twenty-six without realizing she was more than averagely attractive. His lack of interest stung her ego a bit. Perversely, she would have been angry if he had shown a personal attraction. It was irritating to discover that his reaction would have bothered her either way.

"Have a seat, Miss Holland." His low-pitched voice vibrated to her, leaving Deborah with the impression she had been hovering over his desk like some tongue-tied teenager. Which wasn't true at all. She had exhibited both calm and patience.

"Thank you, Mr. Wilding." She let her voice register a courteously polite tone and sat in the straight-back chair positioned to one side of his desk.

Again there was a long pause while he reviewed her application and the remarks noted by her previous interviewers. Deborah wondered if he was deliberately making her wait to make her nervous. She was nervous, but she knew it didn't show.

"You have a bachelor's degree in business administration." The sharp blue eyes glanced at her for confirmation.

"That is correct."

"Your last position was with a travel agency." Before she could acknowledge that, he leaned back in his chair with a ripple of muscle. "You had a wide range of duties and responsibilities with that company. You obtained a good deal of experience in many fields."

"Yes. I have traveled quite extensively in the past six years, taking tours to Europe, the Orient, the Caribbean and South America. Later, I was also responsible for booking tours and arranging accommodations. Through that I became involved in the accounting side and ultimately became more involved in the management side." Deborah briefly mentioned the various roles with the company, knowing the details of each position were spelled out in her résumé.

He didn't look impressed, nor interested in learning more about her previous position. "Were you informed of your results on the typing and shorthand tests that were conducted the day of your first interview?"

"No, I wasn't told my scores." They hadn't concerned her since Deborah was aware she was proficiently skilled in both.

"They were the highest of everyone tested." He imparted the information without a glimmer of a compliment.

"Were they?" she murmured. She hoped she accepted the news without too much smugness.

The tests had been stiff, not the textbook kind. There had been a half hour of steady dictation that had to be translated and typed, as well as a half hour of dictaphone use. It had all been designed to simulate working conditions and not a classroom.

There was a deceptively lazy lowering of his lashes as his eyes narrowed on her. "Your application states that you voluntarily resigned from the travel agency. Why?"

"It is a family-owned company with all the executive positions held by family. There was no room for advancement. I stated my reason in the application."

"The truth please, Miss Holland." His voice was dangerously soft.

"That is the truth, Mr. Wilding." Deborah felt herself bristling at his implication that she was lying, and firmly willed herself to remain calm.

A dark brow arched with taunting skepticism that was both condemning and disdainful. The expensive fabric of his suit was stretched as he reached for another folder on his desk. He set it in front of her. Its tab bore her name.

"We did more than check your references, Miss Holland. We ran a thorough investigation of you. *If* you are offered the position as my personal secretary, you will be privileged to a lot of confidential material. I have to know that you are someone who is reliable and trustworthy." He studied her coldly. "You were engaged to Adam Carter, son and heir apparent of the travel·agency. That engagement was broken. I contend, Miss Holland, that your reasons for leaving were personal and had nothing to do with the lack of advancement potential."

"You are wrong, Mr. Wilding." Her gray eyes smoldered with resentment but she managed to keep the anger out of her voice. "My engagement was broken a year and a half ago, after I realized that marriage with Adam would be a mistake... for both of us. It was a personal decision that did not affect our business relationship. In the past few months I realized I had gone as far as I could go with the company. Higher positions would always be filled by family." Her teeth were on edge as she met his inscrutable look. "If my reasons had been personal, Mr. Wilding, I would have stated that. I certainly wouldn't be ashamed of it or attempt to hide it as you are implying."

The majority of her explanation was true. She omitted the fact that the most serious blow in her broken engagement had been to her pride, rather than her heart. Their relationship had grown out of companionship, business involvement, friendship—a solid foundation, in Deborah's opinion—with passion an incidental sidelight. She had looked the other way when Adam flirted with other women, accepting it as part of his nature. She accepted it until the day she returned early from a meeting and entered her private office to find Adam scrambling off the couch while a red-faced, blond tour guide hastily tried to adjust her blouse.

At the time Deborah had contained her screams of outrage and calmly handed Adam the diamond engagement ring, suggesting that neither of them was ready to get married. She had even smiled politely at the blonde and prompted her to make use of the washroom facilities to repair her smudged makeup.

The whole episode became just one more mark on her love-scarred heart. Like the others, it had healed and toughened her against future romantic flights of fantasy. That's how she could sit across the desk from someone as sexually attractive as the dark-haired man who faced her and not let her imagination run rampant.

"What is your ambition, Miss Holland?" The sideways tilt of his head and the narrowed eyes implied challenge.

"To make the fullest use of my education," Deborah responded without hesitation, sure of herself and her answer. "More specifically, to become a corporate executive."

Her answer appeared to amuse him in a harsh way. "How is the position as my secretary going to help you achieve that goal?"

Deborah suddenly had a picture of herself making coffee all day, as if the job of secretary was a lowly position. "As the position was explained to me, I see it providing me with a broad base of knowledge and experience. Your intricate corporate structure will teach me a great deal about organization and the inner workings of a giant firm. Ambition isn't an exclusively male trait, Mr. Wilding."

"Ambition is often the counterbalance for an unhappy personal life," he remarked and rubbed a hand across his mouth while he considered her coldly.

"That's an interesting theory. My mother always regarded ambition as a means of developing one's potentials to their fullest," Deborah replied, rather than defend the state of her personal life.

His gaze slid from her to the résumé. "Twenty-six. You seem very mature for that age."

It was his attitude rather than his questions that Deborah found so probing. Her previous interviews had been grilling, but here she was being subjected to the third degree. There hadn't been a single question directly related to her qualifications for the job. He was discussing her as a person, examining her under a microscope, and Deborah was finding it a decidedly uncomfortable experience.

"I have been working, earning money since I was eleven. I've been on my own since I was seventeen," she said in explanation.

His gaze briefly flicked to the unopened folder lying on the desk in front of her, the folder carrying the report of his firm's investigation of her. "What about your parents? Are they living?"

Deborah resisted the impulse to ask him why he was bothering with these questions when he knew the answers. "My father died when I was eleven. My mother recently obtained her high school diploma and has enrolled in some night courses. At the moment she works as a hotel maid."

Her voice sounded calm, but she was raging inside. She had struggled to get where she was and she wasn't about to feel shamed by her background. The clothes she wore were modestly expensive, no more charity handouts for her. Money from her savings had provided her mother with an education that had previously been denied her. Deborah was proud of all that she had accomplished, and this arrogant tycoon would not make her feel small for what she had been.

A light glinted in his frosty blue eyes as if he was distantly amused by her surfeit of pride, but otherwise, no emotion registered on the hard features sculpted in bronze. Deborah had heard the term "poker-face" before, but his lack of expression seemed inhuman. It heightened the sensation of danger that played along her nerve ends.

"Any brothers or sisters?"

"Two brothers, both in the air force. My sister was married a month ago. All of them are younger than I am."

"Your sister's wedding—" his lip seemed to curl around the last word, "—was that the reason you quit your last job?"

"I explained my reason for resigning," Deborah reminded him stiffly. "But my sister's wedding did contribute to the timing."

Truthfully, Deborah had felt with her experience

and skills she wouldn't have much difficulty in finding a new and challenging job. Instead, she had found herself losing out because she was overqualified, or else her prospective employers appeared more interested in her looks than her ability. She certainly couldn't accuse Mr. Z. Wilding of the latter.

"And you haven't found another position yet."

"I'm not so desperate for work that I have to take the first job that's offered me." But her savings account was quickly becoming depleted. Soon she wouldn't be able to be that choosy.

"Are you currently living with a man?"

All the questions about her family and home life had lulled her into a false sense of security. Deborah hadn't been prepared for such a personal question. Her gray eyes widened in indignant anger.

"That is none of your business." The question was typical of those put to her by men whose interests were more amorous than professional. "Your only concern about me, Mr. Wilding, is my qualifications for the position." Her sharp voice attempted to put him in his place, but it didn't stir a hair.

"I have no personal interest in your love life, Miss Holland." His low voice carried the ring of steel, without altering its unemotional pitch. "The question is a legitimate one from my viewpoint. The position as my secretary is a demanding one. There are no set hours. You may work from dawn to midnight. I have a grueling schedule that involves a great deal of travel. On occasions, you will be required to accompany me with virtually no advance notice. A lover can create all sorts of complications with demands on your time that conflict with mine."

"And your demands come first," she murmured sweetly, seeing his point but resenting his callous attitude.

"Yes, my demands come first," he agreed with a complacently arrogant smile. "Which is the reason I'm prepared to pay such an exorbitant salary, and why I'm being so selective in my choice. I can't buy a person's loyalty but I can buy his time. If it's knowledge and experience you are seeking, Miss Holland, I can give you both."

Something shivered down her spine. Despite the coldness of the sensation, it heated her flesh. For a fleeting instant, Deborah thought he was referring to sexual knowledge and experience, but there was nothing in his expression or tone to give her that impression. She banished the thought quickly.

"I fully understand your point, Mr. Wilding," she said calmly.

"Good. Someone from my office will be in touch with you soon to inform you of my decision." Abruptly he dismissed her, setting her résumé aside and reaching for the next one.

Deborah sat in stunned silence. Then her natural aggressiveness asserted itself. "How soon, Mr. Wilding? I have received other job offers," she lied, "and don't want to postpone my decision about which to accept because I'm waiting to consider yours." *Put that in your pipe and smoke it*, she thought. Not for anything would she sound over-eager for the job, even if it meant losing it.

He looked up from the résumé with narrowed eyes. "I have no idea how soon. I will not rush my decision. I'll have to take the chance that you might not be available, won't I?'' His sarcasm was thinly veiled.

Deborah took a deep breath and held it, checking her surge of anger. ''Perhaps you could tell me at least how I stack up against my competition?''

At the verb ''stack,'' his gaze seemed to run instinctively over her figure. Despite the vague suggestiveness of it, his attitude was totally impersonal.

''Your skills, education, and experience exceed those of the other applicants. However—'' he paused, the qualifying word stole the satisfaction his initial statement gave her ''—my preference is for a male secretary. Men are more businesslike and less emotional in their approach to work than women.''

''That is a chauvinistic statement if I ever heard one,'' Deborah retorted swiftly. ''Women think more clearly, are more adaptable to new situations and have greater flexibility in their skills.''

He straightened back in his chair, eyeing her with cold disapproval. ''Do you always talk back to your employers?''

''I don't consider it talking back. I prefer to call it speaking out.'' Her fingers gripped the clasp of her purse, but she kept her response even, betraying none of her inner agitation. ''If you are seeking a submissive secretary who will jump when you bark, please withdraw my application from your consideration. I am not a 'yes' person, regardless of how much money I'm paid. If that's what you want, then you don't want me.''

His gaze slid upward to the glint of fire in her mahogany brown hair. ''I already obtained that impression, Miss Holland. As I said, someone from my office will be in touch with you soon." This time the dismissal was final.

Gathering the shreds of her poise, Deborah walked across the length of the room, past the empty desk that shared the room, to the door. Her chance of obtaining this job hovered between slim and none as far as she was concerned. With a sour-grapes attitude, she tried to convince herself it was just as well. Z. Wilding was probably a tyrant. Deborah briefly wondered what the Z. stood for—zero, probably.

In the outer office, Bob Campbell glanced up when she walked in. He scanned her expression through the thick lenses of his glasses. For the first time, Deborah regarded him as a friendly face. His faint smile warmed her after the arctic atmosphere of her interview.

"How did it go?"

She lifted her shoulders in an unknowing shrug and continued to the door as the intercom buzzed. This time, her mouth curved in a wry smile. "Good luck." He would need it. Anyone coming in contact with Z. Wilding would need it.

Stepping into the wide corridor of the office building, Deborah paused to glance at the door. It was marked Private with no other identification of its occupant. The building itself did not carry a name, either outside or on its entrance doors, only its street number. The holding company of LaCosta Enterprises kept a very low profile, as did its owner, Z. Wilding. It would have been a fascinating experience to be a part of it, to learn the true power it wielded behind the scenes. She hadn't been excluded from consideration yet. If she had, Deborah was certain

Mr. Wilding wouldn't have spared her feelings if he believed her unsuitable.

A wishful sigh slipped out as Deborah turned to walk down the long corridor. Outside the building she stopped to put on her sunglasses to shade the glare of the bright Connecticut sun. Her sporty Honda car was parked in the lot. The sleek, little silver and black car had been a present she had given to herself two months after she had broken her engagement to Adam Carter. She needed a job soon if she didn't want the finance company to repossess it. There was enough in her savings to make this month's payment, but next month. . . .

The interior of the car was hot and stuffy from sitting in the sun. The upholstery burned the back of her legs as she slid behind the wheel and hurriedly rolled the windows down. A gentle sea breeze breathed fresh air into the stagnant interior.

Closing the door, Deborah fastened her seatbelt and started the motor. As she backed out of the parking lot and drove forward onto the city streets of Hartford, she paid no attention to the cars buzzing around her. The sporty car zipped through the traffic while its competent driver pulled the pins from her hair and shook its length free of the bun so the wind blowing through the open windows could run its fingers through the burned red strands.

At the apartment complex, Deborah parked her car in the spot reserved for her. She didn't linger in the spring warmth of the afternoon, but hurried up the outside stairs to the second-story entrance of her studio flat.

The combination living room, dining room and

kitchen was decorated in blue and white and silver chrome with an accenting array of potted plants. A teal blue carpet covered the floor in the living area, giving way to white tile streaked with gray and blue in the kitchen. Chrome and glass end tables flanked the sofa upholstered in variegated shades of blue, ranging from blue green to deep peacock blue. Two chairs complemented the sofa in solid shades of light and dark blue. Semiabstract paintings of sea and sky in chrome and black frames adorned the white walls. It was a cool and breezy atmosphere, reflecting the modern tastes and forward-thinking character of its occupant.

Deborah slipped out of her high-heeled shoes and wiggled her nylon-stockinged toes in the plush carpet. The door to the bedroom invited a change of clothes, but she walked to the refrigerator instead. A gallon jar of iced tea sat on the lower shelf. She sat it, and a tray of ice cubes from the freezer section, on the blue formica top of the kitchen counter. She paused to take the receiver of the wall phone from its hook and punched out the number of the employment agency to report the results of her interview.

While it rang, she hunched her shoulder to hold the receiver to her ear, leaving her hands free to open the white-painted cupboard door and remove a glass.

"Mrs. Freeman, please," Deborah requested when the receptionist answered. Two ice cubes clattered into the glass as she was connected with the woman. Deborah juggled the telephone for a moment. "I wanted to let you know that I had my interview."

"How did it go?" The female voice sounded as if she expected the answer to be positive.

"Not too well. They want a man for the job." She overrode her rancor with nonchalance. "I hope you have some other job interviews lined up for me." Balancing the phone on her shoulder again, Deborah filled the glass with the cold tea from the gallon jug.

"Not at the moment." The private employment agent sounded briefly troubled before she forced a brightness into her tone. "But I'm sure we'll find something for you. I'll just have to check my files."

"Of course," Deborah responded dryly. She exchanged a few more courteous phrases with the woman before the conversation ended. As she turned away from the counter, she replaced the receiver on its wall hook and took a sip of her cold drink. The telephone instantly rang. Deborah answered it with a cool, "Hello."

"I didn't know whether you would be home yet or not," her mother's voice came over light, bright and cheery. "I was going to wait until this evening and call before I left for class to find out how your interview went."

"Rotten, if you must know," Deborah sighed.

"Oh." The one word reflected the disappointment the woman felt for her daughter's sake. "What happened?"

"I have the feeling that if I was your son instead of your daughter, I'd be hired now. There is nothing wrong with my qualifications or my experience, except that Mr. Wilding—" she spoke his name with mocking emphasis "—wants a man to fill the job."

"What was he like?" Her mother quietly shifted the subject.

"Arrogant. With about as much feeling as a

stone." Deborah took another swallow of her cold drink.

"He isn't the only pebble on the beach."

Deborah groaned at her mother's attempted joke. "Please." She shook her head wryly. "At the moment his job is the only one in sight. In this instance it's a case of the light at the end of the tunnel is a train. He said I would be contacted soon about his decision, but...." Deborah left the sentence unfinished. "So, how is my college-girl mother?"

"Scared to death that she's going to flunk her tests. I'm not sure I should have let you talk me into these night courses."

There was so much hesitancy and lack of confidence in her mother's voice that Deborah wanted to sigh in frustration. "Don't talk like that. You are very intelligent. You just never had a chance to use it. Don't tell me you want to be a hotel maid all your life?"

"I'm not ashamed of it."

"Neither am I," she asserted. "But look at the way you pushed me to make something of myself. It's my turn to push you."

"In that case you can drive over here this weekend and help me study for the final semester exams," was the answering challenge.

"To tell you the truth, mom, if I don't get a job soon I won't be able to afford the gasoline to drive from Hartford to New Haven," Deborah admitted her growing financial dilemma.

"Is it that bad?" Her mother sounded worried.

"I'll find work," she assured quickly. "It's just I wanted that secretarial position so badly that every other offer has paled in comparison. I just have to stop being so picky.''

"If you need the money, I'll return that check you sent me this month. Art mailed me some money. I can get by—''

"You keep that. If I needed it, I wouldn't have sent it,'' she lied, and immediately seized on the mention of her brother's name to change the subject. "Did Art mention when he'll get some leave? I take it you had a letter from him, which is more than I've had.''

The rest of the conversation became focused on the family; money and finances had no more part in their discussion. Her mother finally became conscious of the length of the long-distance phone call and said goodbye, before her monthly telephone conversation with Deborah became too expensive.

"Relax and enjoy your free time,'' her mother offered in parting.

"Yes, I thought I'd change and go down to the pool,'' Deborah admitted.

"And don't give up hope about that job. That Mr. Wilding might have a change of heart.''

"From granite to marble.''

"Deborah.'' Her mother's tone chided her cynicism.

"I know. I need a good dose of optimism. Bye, mom.''

THE EMPLOYMENT AGENCY had exhausted its supply of job openings that would suit Deborah's qualifications. She didn't have a single interview the rest of the week. On Friday morning she went to buy some

New York newspapers and consider the possibility of moving out of the Hartford area to find work. She was unlocking the door to her apartment when she heard her phone ringing inside. Naturally the key stuck. A few angry curses aided in getting it free and she rushed to answer the phone.

"Ms. Deborah Holland, please," a female voice requested.

"This is she." Part of the thick newspaper slipped from her hand and skittered to the floor.

"Please hold the line while I connect you to Mr. Wilding."

An eyebrow shot up in surprise. The man himself was calling her to deliver the bad news. Deborah hadn't expected that. As a matter of fact, she hadn't expected any notification about the position until the latter part of next week.

A line clicked. "Miss Holland."

It was strange how immediately familiar his voice sounded, cool and commanding, hard like frozen ice. "Yes, sir." She hoped she sounded equally bland.

"Report to my office Monday morning, promptly at seven o'clock."

"Seven o'clock?" It took a second for the implication of his statement to sink in. "This means you are offering me the job."

"I certainly wouldn't waste my time asking you to come to my office on Monday if I intended to offer the position to someone else." His dry taunt mocked her with searing indifference.

Her backbone stiffened at his chiding response. "Am I not allowed any time to consider the job offer before deciding whether to accept it?"

"You have had plenty of time to decide whether or not you would want the position providing it was offered to you, Miss Holland." His tone held little patience. "If you haven't made up your mind by now, then you aren't the person for the job." He paused, and Deborah couldn't think of a single response. "Do you want it or shall I call someone else?"

"I want it, Mr. Wilding," she admitted through her teeth, gritting them until they ached.

"Monday morning. Seven o'clock."

"I'll—" The line was already dead. There was only the hum of the dial tone in her ear.

Deborah glared at the receiver for a frozen instant before slamming it back on its cradle. The newspapers rustled noisily under her feet. There was no need to study the out-of-town classified advertisements. She had work—the position she wanted, but she didn't feel any desire to celebrate.

Bending down, she picked up the newspaper and jammed it in the wastebasket, then walked to her green and blue bedroom to choose her wardrobe for the week ahead. Deborah had no illusions about her new job. Challenging might not be a strong enough word to describe it. And she had no doubt that she would soon find a better word. Z. Wilding would see to that.

CHAPTER TWO

DEMANDING. AFTER ONE FULL WEEK on the job and part of a second, Deborah had found the adjective. From daylight to dusk she had lived, breathed, and eaten LaCosta Enterprises. She had learned, in short order, that her employer tolerated no excuses, not even ignorance. If she didn't know something, someone or someplace, he expected her to find out. Therefore, besides the long hours she put in on the job, Deborah carried home stockholders' reports, corporate analyses of the various firms under the LaCosta banner, résumés of all the corporate executives to familiarize herself with their names and backgrounds, and projections for expansion.

Her duties were many and varied. From such menial tasks as making coffee in the hidden office alcove or acting as chauffeur, they ranged to taking notes at various meetings and conferences. Depending on the confidentiality of the contents, Deborah typed them or the secretary, Mrs. Haines, in the outer office did.

All inner office and inner corporate communication she was to screen, and place on his desk only the important ones. Financial reports, cost sheets, and project estimates were all required to have her opinion attached to them before they were given to him. Half the time Deborah was working in the dark with only rudimentary knowledge of the company or item discussed. When her ignorance surfaced, her employer was quick to point it out—usually in scathing terms.

One thing Deborah had learned—the Z. stood for Zane. The only person she had ever heard address her employer by his given name was Tom Brookshire. He was a quiet, nondescript man with brown hair and eyes, and approximately the same age as Zane Wilding. If Tom had a title, she hadn't discovered it. She had the feeling the two men were longtime friends, not that Zane Wilding ever acted friendly toward anyone. Tom seemed to be his adviser, consultant and right arm. She had the impression he was an attorney, but she hadn't the vaguest idea where his office was located—in the building or elsewhere. Tom just materialized whenever Zand Wilding had need of him. At times it was uncanny.

The column of figures blurred. Deborah paused to rub her eyes tiredly before attempting to find her place and continue rechecking the number totals with her deak calculator. The door to the inner office where she and her employer had their deaks swung open. Deborah glanced up. Only Tom Brookshire entered this private office without being announced or knocking. But it was a petite blonde who walked in. Deborah was too stunned to do more than glance at the dark-haired man behind the large desk.

Zand Wilding, too, had looked up when the door opened, his piercing blue eyes narrowing on the woman who entered. Uncoiling his length from the chair, he stood. Was it her imagination or had she seen a nerve twitch in the hardened line of his jaw? Deborah wondered.

"What are you doing here, Sylvia?"

Nonplussed by the absence of warmth in his greeting, the fragile-looking blonde walked to his desk. There was a haunting delicacy to the profile Deborah viewed. For all the sophistication and elegance of her clothes and hairstyle, the woman had an aura of sensitivity.

"I rode into town with Madelaine and Frank. I thought I would surprise you and give you an opportunity to take your wife to lunch," she announced in a melodic voice.

Wife. That fragile, wandlike creature was his wife. Deborah felt instant pity. Seeing the two of them together with Zane Wilding dominating her with his height and muscled leanness, his rugged countenance so emotionless, it seemed like marrying a child to the devil.

"You should have telephoned to let me know you were coming," he criticized and walked around the desk to loom over her. "I have an important business luncheon today."

Deborah's gray eyes widened at his statement. She had checked his appointment calendar not an hour ago. He had no such engagement. As a matter of fact, he had no meetings until two in the afternoon.

"Oh." The blonde's disappointment was a touching expression. "I suppose it will be one of those long, boring affairs." The wistfulness of her tone hinted that she was saying the words before he did.

"Yes." There wasn't the slightest trace of apology or regret in the cold, bronze features. Strong, male fingers gripped a small-boned elbow to turn the woman from his desk. His intention was obviously to escort her from the room.

But as his wife was turned she saw Deborah seated behind the smaller desk. There was a haunting loveliness to the smile she gave. Deborah was struck by the ivory pallor of the blonde's complexion. She was as pale as if she'd been locked away for several years.

"Is this your new assistant, Zane? You never mentioned that she was so beautiful," she stated without malice or jealousy.

His blue gaze froze for an instant on Deborah's features. "I hadn't noticed." Which was an ego-shattering comment, since Deborah was convinced it was true.

When Zane Wilding showed no inclination to introduce them, Deborah took the initiative. "I'm Deborah Holland."

Limp fingers clasped the hand she extended as the blonde responded with, "I'm Sylvia Wilding." Everything about his wife was so feminine and dainty that Deborah felt like an amazon in comparison.

As the hand was withdrawn, Sylvia Wilding tipped her head sideways to look up to her husband. "You never were attracted to redheads, were you?"

"No, I never have been." There was an underlying tone of impatience in his attitude. Deborah could feel it charging the atmosphere.

His reply was barely out when the door opened and Tom Brookshire walked in. His alert brown gaze quickly took in the situation as he strode forward, a gentle smile spreading across his face. Out of the corner of her eye Deborah saw the hand signal Zane

Wilding made behind his wife's back, indicating he wanted Tom to take his wife from the room.

"Sylvia. This is a surprise." Tom Brookshire sounded genuinely glad to see her. With a natural ease he bent to kiss the blonde's rouged cheek. That display of affection was more than she had received from her husband. "When did you arrive.?"

"Just this minute. How are you, Tom? It seems an age since I saw you last." There was a faint sadness in her smile.

"I'm afraid it has been," he admitted and held both of her hands in his. "You are looking as lovely as ever. What brings you to the city?"

That was another piece of information Deborah hadn't known—where Zane and his wife lived. Obviously it wasn't here in Hartford. Where, she wondered.

"Nothing special. I thought I'd stop and have lunch with Zane," Sylvia began.

"She didn't know I had a luncheon appointment," Zane inserted and the faint emphasis in his voice seemed to prompt a reply from the other man.

"I'm free for lunch. Since Zane can't take you, why don't we sneak away together?" Tom suggested.

"I. . .I'd like that," she agreed after a poignant hesitation.

Tom offered her his arm in a show of gallantry. "Shall we?"

Sylvia Wilding curved a hand inside his arm and paused to glance at Deborah. "It was nice meeting you."

"My pleasure, Mrs. Wilding." Deborah was aware that compassion put added warmth in her response.

As the couple walked from the office, her gray eyes sliced an accusing look to her employer. He was a callous brute, and she seethed at the way he had so coldly palmed off his wife. As if feeling the pricking of the poison darts Deborah was mentally throwing at him, the electric blue of his gaze slid to her.

"If you haven't finished checking those figures, Miss Holland, I suggest you get busy instead of standing around doing nothing."

"Yes, sir," she snapped out the words, venting some of her anger through sarcasm, but it had little effect on him. His skin was much too thick.

The inner office line buzzed on her desk. Returning to her seat in the swivel chair, Deborah punched the lighted button and answered the phone. "Miss Holland's desk."

"This is Mrs. Haines," the secretary in the outer office identified herself. "I'm leaving for lunch now and I wanted you to know that all telephone calls are being switched through your phone."

"Thank you. Have a good lunch."

"Be back in an hour," the older woman promised and hung up.

Only when Mrs. Haines was away from her desk was Deborah responsible for screening the incoming calls for Zane Wilding. The majority of the time she was free from the interruption of a lot of phone calls. Her employer returned calls but rarely accepted any, which necessitated a lot of message taking.

Deborah glanced at the fact sheet she was checking and sighed. It was unlikely she would finish it until after Mrs. Haines returned. Clearing the adding machine, she started the entering of columns of figures into the calculator. With a lead pencil, she made a tiny mark beside each number as she punched it up.

The telephone rang halfway through the column. Deborah let it ring a second time before picking up the receiver. "Mr. Wilding's desk, Miss Holland speaking."

"This is Simpson Armbruster. Is Mr. Wilding in, please?" The male voice held an elderly ring. The name was not one that Deborah remembered hearing mentioned before.

She shot a questioning glance at her employer. Zane Wilding had lifted his head from the report he was reading, his expression an impenetrable bronze mask.

"One moment, Mr. Armbruster." She pressed the hold button, but Zane was already shaking his head to refuse the call. Deborah reconnected the blinking line. "I'm sorry, sir. Mr. Wilding is on another line. May I take a message or have him return your call?" Deborah requested. It hadn't taken her long to invent a variety of excuses why her employer was refusing calls.

Mr. Armbruster asked for his telephone call to be returned and Deborah jotted down the number where he could be reached. When she had hung up the phone, a sun-browned hand was reaching to tear off the sheet of paper with the number. Deborah hadn't realized her employer was anywhere in the vicinity of her desk until that moment, the thick carpet muffling the sound of his approaching footsteps.

He was standing directly behind her chair. There was a rapier thrust of blue steel in the look he gave her. "Did he say why he had called?"

"No. He merely asked you to call him back at your convenience." Everything was always at *his* convenience, she thought, getting a crick in her neck from looking up into his face with its powerful jawline and slanted cheekbones. Out of sheer perversity she added, "Your wife seemed to be a very nice woman... very beautiful."

The steely quality to his blue gaze grew sharper. "I'll return this call from the pool." Pushing back the cuffs of his white shirt and dark jacket sleeve, he glanced at the thin, gold watch on his wrist. "I'll be back at one-thirty."

If he had stated that he wasn't interested in any personal comments from her, Zane Wilding couldn't have made his meaning more clear. As he walked away from her desk toward the door, Deborah studied his lithe, graceful way of moving.

There was so much about him that attracted a woman. The barely tamed thickness of his dull black hair looked feather soft at times. His stature dominated most people he came in contact with and he had the powerfully tapered build of a swimmer, broad muscled shoulders and chest with a flat stomach and slim hips. On the average of three days a week he took a long lunch hour and went to a swimming pool in the vicinity to exercise, Deborah had learned. That, no doubt, accounted for his excellent physical condition in spite of the hours spent behind the desk.

There was so much virility in his rugged features cast in bronze that Deborah wondered why she had gained the impression of unfulfillment from his wife. A woman as feminine as she was should appeal to a man as masculine as Zane Wilding. His chiseled mouth had made no attempt to kiss his wife, not even with a chaste peck. But Deborah remembered that she had never seen him exhibit even a normal interest in the opposite sex. Somehow she found it difficult to reconcile his attitude of iron celibacy to the male lust that she suspected seethed behind that bronze armor of indifference.

Taking a firm grip on her wandering thoughts, Deborah shook away the half-formed curiosity about her employer's love life. Whom he slept with—or didn't sleep with—wasn't her concern. Zane Wilding would be the first one to tell her so, if he knew.

AFTER A MONTH, Deborah's life settled into a routine. The only thing routine about her job was the lack of a set routine, other than work. Her duties weren't restricted to the office. Four times she had attended business dinners with her employer where she was required to take mental notes of the discussion and transcribe a generalized account of the meeting into a report that she submitted to Zane Wilding the next afternoon. Fortunately, after these late night dinners she wasn't required to be in the office until noon the next day, but she usually spent the free mornings jotting down her recollections of the previous night's conversations so they could be organized into a report when she reached the office.

There were two out-of-town trips in the first month, one to New York and the other to Los Angeles. The first time Tom Brookshire had flown with them, but the second time it was only Deborah and her employer. If it had been anyone other than

Zane Wilding, Deborah would have been wary of spending two or three nights in the same hotel as her boss. But she could have had three eyes and one leg for all the notice Zane Wilding paid to her. Everything was strictly business.

In all the long hours they had spent together, he had never made any comment that could be construed as friendly or personal. All the words that came out of his mouth were orders, commands or requests. On rare occasions he opened a door for her or held a chair, but Deborah could count those times on her fingers. They were the only times that he revealed he was aware of the fact she was a member of the female sex.

Once or twice the feminine part of her makeup wanted to rebel at his indifferent treatment of her, but Deborah always quelled the revolt. Theirs was a business relationship—employer and employee. It wouldn't be wise to complicate it, she realized.

The job was living up to all her expectations of being exposed to the many and varied facets of a large corporation. However questionable her opinion was of Zane Wilding as a human being, Deborah had no reservations about his skill as a businessman. His experience and natural acumen were beyond hers. He seemed born to command. She doubted that there were many men who could sit silently through an entire meeting and still be totally in charge of all that was discussed—as he was doing now.

Her gray eyes glanced absently from her shorthand note pad and its record of the discussion to the strong, lean hands on her right. They were male hands with blunted nails and wisps of dark hair curling from beneath white shirt cuffs. Beneath the sun-browned skin there was the tensile strength of steel. They were the hands that firmly held the reins of a multimillion-dollar conglomerate.

Thumbing to the next page of the report, he lifted a hand to rub a knuckle against the hard line of his mouth in aloof concentration. Deborah found herself wondering how often the inherent mastery in his touch was directed into a caress. She had never met a man who exhibited less need for human contact than Zane Wilding did.

One of the double doors to the large conference room was opened a crack. Deborah saw Mrs. Haines peer hesitantly in. The interruption drew a slicing look of censure from Zane. As unobtrusively as possible, Deborah rose from her chair and walked quietly to the door.

"What is it, Mrs. Haines?" she whispered.

The older woman wore an apologetic, yet agitated look. "It's Mrs. Wilding on the phone."

"Which line?"

"Two."

"Thank you, Mrs. Haines." Deborah smiled firmly and closed the door.

Before the meeting had begun, Zane Wilding had left strict orders to hold all calls. With that indelibly imprinted in her mind, Deborah walked to the telephone on the small table in the corner of the room. She pushed the button to connect the second line and picked up the receiver.

"Mrs. Wilding? This is Miss Holland." She kept her voice low so as not to intrude on the discussion going on behind her at the long table.

"I don't want to talk to you! I asked to speak to Zane. Where is he?" There was a slurred pattern to the strident female voice. Deborah found little resemblance between the quiet-spoken blonde she had met in the office and the agitated woman on the line.

"I'm sorry. He's in a conference right now. Let me have him call you back in an hour," Deborah suggested.

"Conference! He isn't in any conference. You're lying to me!"

"I assure you, Mrs. Wilding—"

"You damned little bitch!" It was becoming more and more apparent that Sylvia Wilding was drunk. "He's with you right now, isn't he? What's he doing? Making love to you? Is he kissing you and fondling you? You cheap little slut, I bet you think it's funny to be talking to me while he's holding you in his arms."

The flurry of jealous accusations momentarily shocked Deborah. "Mr. Wilding is chairing a corporate meeting at this moment." The denial came out in a breathless rush of indignation.

"Chairing a meeting? Hah! He's bedding you. Do you like all that naked muscle against your skin? I'll bet you want to have his baby."

"Please—" There didn't seem to be anything she could say to stop this torrent of suggestive questions.

"I want to speak to Zane! You put him on the phone this instant!"

"Who are you speaking to, Miss Holland?" The harsh demand came from Zane Wilding.

Clamping a hand over the mouthpiece of the receiver, Deborah half turned to answer him. "It's your wife."

But the hand covering the mouthpiece didn't stop the stream of abusive and obscene language that echoed into the room. And all those vilely suggestive comments were directed at Deborah. The red stain of embarrassment heated her face as she became the cynosure of all eyes in the room.

Anger blazed with hot flames in Zane Wilding's eyes. Deborah sensed the severely suppressed violence as he uncoiled his length from the chair and crossed the room to yank the receiver from her hand.

"I'm here, Sylvia. This is Zane. Everything's all right now. Settle down," he ordered.

At the same instant that he spoke, Tom Brookshire was rising from his chair and quietly ushering the other men from the room. No one questioned his reason. Deborah was conscious of the executive staff leaving, but she was rooted to the floor by the foul things Sylvia Wilding had said to her. Deborah waited expectantly for her employer to leap to her defense and refute all the vile accusations.

As Zane became aware of her continued presence beside him, he turned and gestured to Tom to take her out of the room. His look was cold when it glanced off her, his eyes the deep arctic blue of a glacier. Deborah was stunned by his attitude.

As Tom took hold of her arm to lead her away, she heard Zane say to his wife, "Don't be ridiculous. I have never refused to take a call from you. If anyone claims I did, they're lying. Where is Madelaine?" Ignoring Deborah's outraged look at the implication in his words that labeled her a liar, Zane covered the receiver and issued a sharp order to Tom, "She says she doesn't know where Madelaine is. Try the other estate number. If you can't get anybody, patch Armbruster onto this line."

"Right."

Tom didn't take any notice of Deborah's stiffness as he escorted her from the conference room. Outside, Mrs. Haines had commandeered a typist's desk and was using the phone. She looked up anxiously when Tom stopped at her chair.

"I can't get any answer at the other number," she informed him.

"Keep trying." His fingers remained firmly on Deborah's elbow as he walked to an adjoining desk. "Take a coffee break," he told the young typist and glanced at her coworkers in the room trying not to show their interest in what was happening. In a louder voice Tom ordered, "Everyone take a twenty-minute break."

As the typing pool was cleared, Deborah muttered angrily beneath her breath, "I have never been so humiliated in all my life. She had no reason to speak to me like that. Everyone in the whole room heard what she said."

Tom's mouth slanted in a wry smile. "Sooner or later everyone in the company will begin speculating about whether you and Zane are having an affair. Sylvia just put the thought in their minds that much quicker." He picked up the telephone and tapped out a number on the push buttons.

Tom's reply didn't do anything to cool the heat in her cheeks. "They can speculate all they like and it will still be absurd. That arrogant—" Deborah checked the word that trembled on the edge of her tongue. "He practically called me a liar, when he had made it very plain that he wanted all calls held while he was in that meeting.''

"All calls do not include ones from his wife. They are put through to him, regardless," Tom informed her.

"No one told me that," she retorted.

"That's unfortunate," he admitted, then turned his attention to the receiver in his hand. "Yes, Armbruster. Sylvia's on another line. Hold on while I patch you through." After a hurried consultation with the operator, Tom made the connection between the two lines and hung up his receiver. The tense lines of concern that had etched the corners of his mouth, went away as he sighed and turned his attention back to Deborah. His gaze lightly scanned the indignant thinness of her lips and the silvery lights glittering angrily in her gray eyes. "Don't take the things Sylvia said to you too personally."

"Too personally?" Her scoffing laugh was harsh. "I have never been made to feel so cheap in all my life. A sailor would have turned red at some of her language."

"Yes...." Tom paused to take a deep breath, an action that seemed weary. "Sylvia can't be held responsible for what she does...or says."

"If you mean simply because she was drunk, I should ignore—"

"Sylvia is an alcoholic," Tom interrupted.

"I didn't know." Deborah frowned. "I didn't guess. When she was in the office—"

"She happened to be sober that time." He sat his lanky frame on the edge of the desk, hooking a leg over the corner. "Zane doesn't talk about it, but I'm not telling you anything that isn't common knowledge to the other members of his private staff. Since you are now a part of the team you might as well know, too."

"I see," she murmured, her feeling of outrage slowly dissolving.

"I've known Sylvia almost as long as I've known Zane. She was never a very emotionally stable girl. Her moods fluctuated from very high to very low. After Ethan drowned, she fell apart."

"Ethan? What was Ethan?"

"Their son. He was only four years old. Sylvia was in a doctor's care for several months after his death. She blamed herself for the accident. He was out playing by the river and fell into the water. Sylvia had been reading not far away while he played. She heard him scream, but by the time she reached the riverbank he'd gone under. She was hysterical when Zane finally found her wading along the river searching for Ethan's body. That was fourteen years ago."

"But hasn't anyone tried to—" Deborah stopped, hesitant that she might be asking questions that weren't any of her business.

"I don't know how many times Zane has had her dried out, but it rarely lasts longer than a month before she goes on another binge. Obviously that's what happened today. Sometimes she just cries and other times she makes a lot of wild accusations against friends and relatives alike. There have been occasions when she gets drunk and doesn't say a word for days, just walks around in a stupor. It's pitiful, really."

"Yes, I can see that," Deborah nodded.

The conference-room door opened and Zane stepped out. He glanced around the empty and virtually silent typing pool, before his grim look stopped on Tom.

"Have somebody bring in a fresh pot of coffee and tell the others we will resume the meeting in fifteen minutes," he ordered. His hard gaze burned to Deborah. "Come in here, Miss Holland."

Uncertainty flickered across her expression as she glanced at Tom, but he was already straightening from the desk to carry out Zane's request. Deborah had no idea what she had done to spark his obvious displeasure, but she wasn't about to let him intimidate her with his glowering expression. Carrying herself with determined poise, Deborah walked past Zane into the empty conference room and left him to close the door behind her.

"Would you explain to me what the hell you were trying to prove by refusing that phone call?" With hardly a break in stride, he made his tight-lipped demand and swept past her to the chair at the head of the long conference table.

"What I was trying to prove!" Her temper ignited and she tried to bank the heat of her anger. "I was following the instructions you left to hold all calls. I wasn't aware that the restriction didn't include your wife!"

"Now you are. I don't want a repeat of this incident," he snapped and picked up the opened report lying on the table.

"You don't want a repeat of this! I can assure you neither do I!" Deborah flared.

His gaze lifted from the papers to study impassively the storm clouds in her look. "Are you expecting an apology for what happened?" There was a menacing quality to the softly spoken question.

"I don't think it would be asking too much," she retorted.

"If I began apologizing for every time my wife made an ass of herself, I would be doing it the rest of my life. Now that you are aware of the type of treatment you can expect to receive from my wife, you have a choice of either accepting it or leaving," he challenged with cold indifference.

"Just like that," she breathed in enraged astonishment.

"I'm not about to pander to your ego, Miss Holland. If you can't take a few insults from a drunk, I have no use for you. You'd better learn to roll with the punches, even the low blows, or you'll never make it in this organization. Make up your mind. You either stay or you go. I only have room in my life for one paranoid female."

Pressing her lips into a thin line, Deborah turned on her heel and walked to the corner table where she had left her pencil and note pad beside the telephone. With these in hand, she returned to the chair she had occupied on Zane Wilding's left and sat down. Through her actions, she gave him her decision. His expressionless blue eyes took note of the fact, but he made no comment.

CHAPTER THREE

"My, but it is humid this evening." The sophisticated brown-haired woman leaned closer to the long mirror and pressed powder on her shiny nose and cheeks. A huge diamond cocktail ring on her finger caught fire in the artificial light.

"Yes, it is." Deborah was seated on one of the pink velvet-covered stools in the elegant powder room of the exclusive restaurant. She took her time freshening her lipstick as her gray eyes flickered to the manicured reflection of Mrs. Darrow, wife of a well-known financier. He was vacationing in Florida, hence the flying business trip to Tampa to meet with him.

"I have tried to convince Bianca that it would be much too warm to dine on the lanai this evening." The woman's glance strayed to her daughter standing next to her, fluffing her long chestnut curls. "But she thought it would be so romantic. It was a very evocative setting, but I feel so sticky now."

"Yes." Deborah blotted her lips with a tissue.

What had started out to be a business dinner to persuade the financier, Foster Darrow, to back a large land development project LaCosta Enterprises had in the works, had rapidly deteriorated into a social event. Instead of it being a quiet dinner between the financier and Zane with Deborah and Mrs. Darrow sitting on the sidelines, the man had brought his nineteen-year-old daughter along. She was a beautiful girl with glossy chestnut hair and golden tanned skin. Within minutes after being introduced to Zane she had made her interest in him quite obvious. At virtually the same instant, Zane had excused himself to find out what was delaying Tom Brookshire.

To Deborah's knowledge there had been no mention of Tom's being included in the evening's discussion. Fifteen minutes later, Tom had joined them and immediately began exuding his quiet charm on the daughter, distracting her attention from Zane. It hadn't taken Deborah long to realize that her employer was using Tom as a buffer to keep the aggressive young girl at bay.

She felt sorry for Bianca Darrow, but part of her understood the attraction the girl felt for the aloof, dark man. His remoteness and air of indifference toward the opposite sex challenged a woman to be the one he noticed. Couple that with his severely handsome looks and latent virility and it made a very potent combination.

"I don't know how many times I've told Foster that we have no business coming to Florida in July. The climate is so tropical that it's oppressive in the summer," Mrs. Darrow declared.

"Tonight is an exception," Deborah defended without rancor. "Usually the Gulf breezes keep it from becoming too steamy."

"Have you lived here long?" The faintly brittle question came from Bianca Darrow.

"I live in Connecticut."

"How long have you worked for Zane?" A pair of youthfully haughty brown eyes swept over Deborah's reflection, as if assessing her competition.

Her copper-tipped lashes veiled the dry humor the girl's look prompted. Deborah could have told the girl that she had nothing to worry about from her. If she had been a robot, Zane Wilding couldn't have shown less interest in her personal life. He didn't even recognize that she had one. The distantly polite smiles Bianca Darrow had received tonight were more than Deborah had seen in all the time she had been working for Zane Wilding. And none of them had ever been directed at her.

"I've been in Mr. Wilding's employ for a little over three months now," Deborah answered and absently smoothed her dark copper hair at the sides, checking to be sure no wisp had escaped the sleek coil at the nape of her neck.

"Did you know him before?" The young brunette wandered over to stand behind Deborah.

"No." Deborah noticed how much her suntan had faded. The long working hours that sometimes included the weekends, had deprived her of free time to spend lazing in the Connecticut summer sun. Compared to Bianca Darrow, she looked pale, her complexion the color of golden cream framed by the burnt copper shade of her hair.

"It's a shame about his wife," Bianca commented in a probing fashion. "Do you know her?"

"I met Mrs. Wilding once," Deborah admitted and offered no more than that.

"From all I've heard, she must be an ill woman,"

Mrs. Darrow inserted. Deborah had suspected the woman had a gossiping nature and wondered how she could get out of this conversation. "It can't be a happy marriage. I'm surprised he hasn't divorced her after all this time."

"I image Mr. Wilding feels she is his wife—in sickness and in health." Deborah slipped the tube of lipstick into her small purse. Truthfully, she didn't know what his feelings were toward his wife, or even if he had any.

"No one would blame him if he divorced her and tried to find happiness with someone else," Bianca stated with a faintly wistful look in her brown eyes.

"No one would blame him," Deborah agreed dryly. "But I don't think Mr. Wilding would be concerned if they did."

"Has Zane ever indicated to you that he was considering a divorce?" the girl questioned.

"I am merely one of his business aides. Mr. Wilding doesn't discuss his personal affairs with me." Deborah put faint stress on the formal term of address, seeking to emphasize her point that her relationship to Zane Wilding involved only business.

The girl turned to her mother. "I don't think he lets it show, but I'm certain Zane is a very lonely man."

If he was, Deborah thought to herself, it was by choice. There were probably a lot of attractive women, like Bianca Darrow, who were eager to console him. Perhaps he had a mistress or two hidden away, although Deborah didn't know when he ever found the time to see them. Her own social life had become practically nonexistent since she had gone to work for him.

Glancing at her reflection in the full-length mirror, Deborah ran an adjusting hand around the ruffed neckline of her white silk blouse. It was discreetly scooped to show off the cameo necklace resting near the hollow of her throat. Her narrowly pleated skirt in a green and white pattern almost touched the floor, belted at the waist to accent its slimness. Deborah never dressed to draw attention to herself, but the simple styles always succeeded in pointing out her natural assets rather than downplaying them.

"It must be wonderful to work so closely with Zane," Bianca remarked with a trace of envy.

"It's very challenging," Deborah altered the meaning without disagreeing with the young woman. She knew what a hard taskmaster her employer was. But Bianca Darrow's rose-colored view had painted him as a very romantic figure and she would never have accepted Deborah's opinion of the driving, emotionless side she had been exposed to. "Shall we rejoin the others in the lounge?" she suggested.

"We should, yes," Mrs. Darrow glanced and laughed with shrill gaiety. "Of course, Foster is used to waiting for me, but I imagine Zane is an impatient man."

Deborah didn't comment on that as she led the way out of the ladies' powder room to the dimly lighted lounge. A small band was playing a slow number for a handful of couples on the dance floor. At their approach, the three men rose courteously to seat them. Deborah walked around the table to take the chair between her employer and the financier. It was her usual position at most informal meetings, permitting her to take mental notes of what Zane Wilding said and the response he received. She doubted that there would be much business discussion this evening, though.

In a strictly polite gesture, Zane Wilding pulled her chair away from the small circular table. Her absent smile was equally automatic, with no more meaning than his action. As she moved to the front of the chair and lifted her long skirt out of the way, he inclined his head slightly toward her.

"I have already ordered you an after-dinner drink. A Drambuie," he informed her in a low tone. "Is that acceptable?"

"Yes." She paused to answer him, turning her head to look at him when she did.

"Listen to that music, Zane." Bianca Darrow had walked to the chair on the other side of Zane, a position that put her between him and Tom Brookshire. There was an effusive, happy sound to her comment. "Doesn't it make you want to dance?" Her question angled for an invitation.

Indifferent to the young woman's obvious attempts to gain her employer's attention, Deborah started to sit down. A strong, male hand clamped itself on her wrist to stop the movement. Startled by the knowledge the hand belonged to Zane Wilding, her questioning eyes darted to the impenetrable mask of his dark features. His next words surprised her even more than the unexpectedness of his touch.

"As a matter of fact, it does," he agreed smoothly with Bianca's remark. "I just asked Miss Holland to have this dance with me. You will excuse us."

The last comment was directed to everyone at the table.

Concealing her astonishment and ignorance of any invitation, Deborah managed to close her mouth before she was led away from the table to the dance floor. Just as Tom had been used as a buffer, her presence was being utilized to keep the young woman at a distance. Deborah didn't think for one minute that Zane Wilding was doing it because he couldn't deal with Bianca Darrow's blatant pursuit. She suspected that he was avoiding any rude confrontation that might offend the girl's father. It was a rare show of diplomacy from a man whom Deborah had been accustomed to hearing bluntly speak his mind. She saw the bitter flash of jealousy in Bianca's look as Zane guided her to the dance floor.

An odd feeling of self-consciousness attacked Deborah when he shifted his hold on her wrist and placed a hand on the curve of her waist. The other couples dancing to the slow music were almost melted together, but at least six inches separated Deborah from the leanly muscled build of her partner. His steps followed a basic pattern that was easy to follow, although the hand at her waist made sure of it by firmly directly her movements to match his.

Deborah wasn't sure which was more unnerving—being held so firmly at a distance as Zane was doing now, or being held close to the hard male body inches from her own. Either way, the situation made her feel on edge. The warmth in the strong fingers clasping hers brought a tightness to her throat. Her gaze focused itself on an imaginary point on his right shoulder, rather than lift the few inches necessary to study his face at close quarters.

Just the same she was conscious of his slanted jawline and strong chin on a level somewhere near her forehead, and the chiseled contours of his mouth above that. The clean, manly fragrance of his shaving cologne dominated her sense of smell and disturbed her breathing.

The music and the intimacy implied in dancing together were making her reaction to his nearness much too physical. Deborah realized that was dangerous ground. It became imperative to speak and assert the business footing of their relationship again.

"This hasn't been a very productive evening, has it?" she remarked in what she hoped was a calm voice.

"Wasted would be a more accurate description." His low-pitched voice triggered pleasant vibrations through her bones, despite the grimness of his tone.

Fighting back that reaction, Deborah quipped, "Not totally wasted. The food was good."

She lifted her gaze a few inches and saw his mouth quirk at her statement. It was the closest she had ever come to receiving a smile from her taciturn employer. Of course, the dry expression never reached the steel-blue depths of his eyes. Deborah was convinced nothing ever did.

His impersonal gaze briefly skimmed her length. "Didn't you wear this same outfit two weeks ago when we dined with the president of the architectural firm?"

Discovering that he actually noticed what she wore was a pleasant revelation. It gleamed in her clear, gray eyes. "Yes, I did," she admitted.

Immediately his blue eyes narrowed to a piercing degree. "I suppose you have a limited choice of evening wear, which is why you have to keep wearing the same things over and over.".

Deborah realized that she had mistakenly interpreted his first remark as a compliment. "A very limited choice," she replied stiffly. "It consists of one dress, one pantsuit, an evening gown, and this. None of them is very extravagant, but then I'm not taking part in a fashion parade. I have other things to spend my money on besides evening clothes to entertain your business associates." Silver lightning flashed in her eyes, crackling with her temper.

"Something will have to be done to enlarge your wardrobe." His tone indicated an impatience that he had to be bothered with such a minor detail.

"May I suggest, Mr. Wilding, that you give me a raise and arrange to let me have some free time while the shops are open so I can correct the situation?" Deborah was practically steaming, resenting his criticism of her limited wardrobe.

"Are you complaining about your salary and long hours?" A black eyebrow lifted in challenge.

"You are the one who is complaining—about my limited evening wear. I was offering a remedy." She gave him a saccharine smile.

"I see." There was a glint in his eye that suspiciously resembled amusement.

Deborah looked away, preferring his frigid regard to silent, mocking laughter. Her gaze touched on other dancing couples, entwined in each other's arms. The distance between them made her feel conspicuous. Not that she wanted to rest her head on that chest of living stone, because she had no amorous inclinations for her employer. But she was aware that the firm warmth of the hand at her back and the fingers curved around her own, were at odds with his attitude of chilling indifference. She stifled that knowledge, not knowing where it might lead.

"It's unfortunate that you aren't as quick to praise as you are to criticize, Mr. Wilding," she issued tightly, looking anywhere but at her employer and his carved face that was not that far from her own. "Because it seems impossible to satisfy you."

"You can be assured, Miss Holland, that if you do something that doesn't satisfy me, I'll let you know." Dry amusement lurked in his low voice.

Flashing gray eyes swung back to meet his gaze. "Which is precisely my point. A person is just as eager to find out when she does something right as she is to know when she's wrong."

"So you want me to say you've done an excellent job so far."

"No, I don't want you to say it," she denied. "I want you to mean it. Praise is worth nothing when it's prompted."

"I'm surprised you know that," he murmured in a faintly superior tone.

Deborah gritted her teeth. "I knew working for you was going to be an experience, but I didn't realize it was going to be a lesson in male arrogance."

The arm at her waist tightened to turn her away from a couple who would have danced blindly into them. Briefly Deborah felt the contact with his muscled thigh. It was a jolting reminder of the lean, hard length of a man in his prime. After that, she kept her mouth closed rather than have Zane Wilding think she was attempting to attract his attention to her femininity. When the song ended, she escaped the unnerving indifference of his arms and turned to walk back to the table. Naturally he was right behind her.

His low, bland voice taunted, "Unprompted, may I state that your silence was refreshing."

Deborah flashed him a glance over her shoulder and met the hard, cold blue of his eyes. "You may state anything you wish. You are the boss." Satisfied that she had the last word, she fixed a calmly pleasant expression on her face and continued to the table where the others waited for them.

Ignoring the speculative looks from the financier and his wife, and the jealous green of their daughter's, Deborah walked to her chair. Zane Wilding was there to pull it out for her and she caught the curious, assessing look Tom Brookshire gave him.

"Thank you for the dance, Miss Holland." The glinting light in his blue eyes was challenging and hard.

A sharp retort trembled on her lips that she hadn't been given the opportunity to refuse, but she bit it back and nodded with thinly faked courtesy. While he took the chair beside her, Deborah reached for her drink to cover her tense unease.

"You made a charming couple on the dance floor, Miss Holland," the florid-faced Mr. Darrow remarked.

"Oh." She glanced at the financier over the rim of her glass. "Obviously you didn't notice how many times I stepped on Mr. Wilding's toes." *Figuratively, at least,* she thought, and glanced across the table to see the raised eyebrow of Tom Brookshire whose expression was a combination of amusement and sharp question.

Thankfully, no one pursued her comment as Bianca Darrow spoke to draw Zane Wilding's attention to her and away from Deborah. Not once during the course of the evening did her employer ask either Mrs. Darrow or her daughter to dance. Deborah expected them to be offended by his slighting of them, but except for the jealous looks Bianca kept casting her way, neither woman appeared angry over the lack of an invitation.

The financier asked Deborah to dance once, after he dutifully danced first with his wife and later her daughter. On the floor he confessed to Deborah that he preferred to polka. She surmised his preference was the reason he kept pumping her arm while they danced to a slow tune. It was probably an unconscious effort to speed up the tempo of the song. Whatever his reason, her arm practically ached by the time the song ended. At the table Deborah kept her mouth firmly shut most of the time, not speaking unless a remark was addressed specifically to her. Having stuck her foot in her mouth once that evening, she had no intention of repeating it. Besides, if Zane Wilding found her silence refreshing, she decided he could freeze in it.

When Tom led her onto the dance floor near the end of the evening, he commented on her subdued behavior. "You are awfully quiet tonight, Deborah."

"Don't you find my silence refreshing?" The caustic challenge was out before she could stop it.

Automatically his gaze shifted to Zane Wilding seated at the table. He didn't need to be told who had prompted that remark.

"I'm sorry, Tom," Deborah apologized stiffly. "I had no reason to snap at you."

"But you've been snapping at him," he guessed, a smile twitching his mouth.

"He was complaining that I wear the same evening clothes all the time. Working eighteen hours a day, seven days a week for him," Deborah exaggerated in anger, "when do I have time to buy anything new? I don't like being unfairly criticized and I told him so." An astute pair of brown eyes flicked to the dark copper sheen of her hair. Deborah noticed it and simmered. "Don't go blaming the sharpness of my tongue on red hair. My sister has fiery red hair and she's as timid as a church mouse. I've always been independent and outspoken."

"I didn't say a word." Tom drew his head back in mock defense.

It was just the right attitude to cool her seething temper. "I snapped again, didn't I?" she smiled ruefully and sighed.

"Don't worry about it." He dismissed her need to apologize. His calmness in the face of her stormy resentment toward their mutual employer had a stabilizing effect and brought an end to her silent, bristling attitude.

It took the acrid taste out of the evening, letting it

end on a peaceful note. But it was part of Tom's job to smooth the feathers his boss might have ruffled. Deborah had realized that a long time ago.

BECAUSE OF THE LATE FLIGHT back to Connecticut, Deborah wasn't required to come into the office until ten the next morning. Passing through the outer office, she tossed a "good morning" to the efficient, prim secretary guarding the door to the private domain of her employer. Zane Wilding was on the telephone when she walked in. Her gaze took note of the fact as she continued toward her desk.

Cupping a hand over the mouthpiece, he glanced at her. "What are your measurements, Miss Holland?"

The question stopped her dead. "I—beg your pardon?" The phrase tumbled out in an astonished breath.

"Your measurements, what are they?" he repeated curtly.

Deborah stiffened. "I don't see that it's any of your business."

His mouth thinned into an even harder line. Removing his hand, he spoke into the phone. "Hold the line, please." He punched the red hold button and lifted his head to regard her with icy-blue indifference. "I'm having some evening clothes sent to your apartment to supplement your wardrobe. I could guess at your size, but it would be much simpler if you gave me your measurements, your height and your weight."

His sweeping gaze mentally stripped away her loose-fitting blouse and her side-split skirt of khaki, and assessed the flesh-and-bone contours of her figure. Self-consciousness flamed her skin at his thorough inspection. Despite the analytical quality of his look, his inherent virility gave it overtones of sexual interest.

"It isn't necessary for you to arrange anything," Deborah refused his offer. "I'll take care of my wardrobe myself."

"As you pointed out, both your time and your money are limited," he replied with a scant effort at patience. "Since it's unlikely that you will ever have a personal need for an extensive array of evening dresses, and since I have required that you obtain one to fulfill your position, it's reasonable that I should furnish you with the additional clothes. I am merely furnishing an employee with a uniform that I deem necessary. Is that clear?"

"Perfectly," she agreed rigidly.

"Then please oblige me by giving your vital statistics." It was an order, a demand, but not a request.

Struggling to keep her poise, Deborah responded. "I'm five foot seven, 125 pounds, with measurements of 35-25-36."

Without a flicker of an eye, Zane Wilding repeated the numbers over the telephone and added, "She has dark auburn hair and gray eyes. I'll trust you to make the appropriate choices, including accessories. If any of them prove unsatisfactory, they will be returned. Send the bill to my attention." When the conversation was ended, he hung up the receiver. Deborah was still standing in the center of the room. His gaze skimmed her face briefly. "You are looking pale, Miss Holland. You need some sun."

Her temper simmered as she realized his criticism of her appearance wasn't over yet. "When would you suggest I do that, Mr. Wilding, when I spend every daylight hour inside these four walls?" Her question was deliberately sarcastic.

But he was unscathed by her sharpness. "Try a sunlamp then." He began shifting through the papers stacked in front of him to resume his morning reading of a half dozen of the leading newspapers across the country.

"Is that what you do?" Her glittering gray eyes took in the sun-bronzed features so vital and disgustingly healthy in their color.

"I have in the past," he admitted, giving her a considering look. "However, if you want access to the pool facilities I make use of during the lunch hour, you have only to ask. The exercise would probably do you good with as much sitting around as you do."

At that moment, Deborah fervently wished they were at the swimming pool so she could have the pleasure of pushing him in. Instead, she kept a rein on her temper and walked to her desk without responding to his suggestion. The problem was he was so often absolutely right in his judgments and solutions that it infuriated Deborah.

IT WAS DARK by the time she left the office that day and drove to her apartment. Dress boxes were stacked on her teal blue carpet, bearing the scrolled name of a well-known fashion shop in the city. Deborah stared at them resentfully for a minute, then kicked off her shoes and began opening them.

By the time she had finished, mounds of protective

tissue paper were piled on the floor and an array of evening gowns and cocktail dresses adorned the sofa. The understated simplicity of the clothes emitted a subdued elegance that made them reek of money. All the colors were designed to complement her unusual combination of auburn hair and gray eyes. The accessories ran the range from designer shoes to scarves and evening shawls.

Deborah could find fault with only one choice. A scarlet cocktail dress with threads of silver would make too flamboyant a combination with her red hair. That she set aside to be returned to the store. After trying on three and discovering they were a perfect fit, she didn't bother with the other dozen that remained.

Her clothes closet hadn't been filled before. Now she found herself taking things out to make room for the expensive gowns. The task meant rearranging and cleaning out all the drawers of her bedroom bureau in order to find a place to put the clothes she had taken out of the closet. It was nearly midnight before her apartment was restored to some semblance of order and she was able to tumble into her bed and fall into an exhausted sleep.

As usual, when she arrived at the office early the next morning, Zane Wilding was already there. Deborah informed him that the evening dresses had been delivered and that she was returning one as unsatisfactory to her needs, but she didn't thank him for his generosity in the number or costliness of them. She argued with herself that to feel gratitude was wrong. After all, he had been the one who was dissatisfied with her appearance.

The following week there was another late-evening business dinner that she was required to attend. Deborah wore one of the new gowns, a simple yet sophisticated design fashioned in silver lamé. It was highly complimentary to her coloring. Tom Brookshire was quick to tell her how attractive she looked, but there wasn't a single remark from Zane Wilding about her appearance. If it hadn't been for a cursory, sweeping glance from those arctic-blue eyes, Deborah might have thought he hadn't noticed the new dress. It was an effort to smother her irritation with him, but she eventually succeeded and concentrated on taking mental notes of the conversation that ensued.

CHAPTER FOUR

DEBORAH WASN'T SURE what had wakened her, but it hadn't been the buzz of the alarm clock on the bedside table. She stretched lazily and yawned before glancing at the clock's face. Half-past seven it read, and she jumped out of bed in panic, grabbing for the clock. The stem of the alarm hadn't been completely pulled out so the buzzer hadn't gone off.

"Damn, damn, damn," she swore softly as she raced for the bathroom.

Some inner sense had warned her subconscious of the lateness of the hour and wakened her. But she wouldn't have time for any breakfast, not even a cup of instant coffee. She had under thirty minutes to dress and drive to the office, a combination that usually took an hour.

Swiping a brush over her teeth, Deborah promised them a better cleaning that night. She slapped on some lipstick and ran a brush through her hair. There wasn't time to style it in its efficient bun so she let its waving curls tumble around her shoulders. Pulling a shapeless, ocher-colored dress over her head, she grabbed a belt from the closet and a pair of shoes. As she hurried out her apartment door, she was fastening the belt while juggling her purse, shoes, and the amended report for the business meeting scheduled promptly for nine that morning.

The traffic that September day was heavy. Usually she left early enough to miss the rush, but this time she was caught in the middle of people on their way to work and parents driving their children to school. The frustration of having to poke along when every part of her screamed to hurry worked on her nerves. Her fingers drummed on the steering wheel.

The traffic light at the intersection just ahead of her changed to yellow. Deborah considered trying to speed through the caution light before it changed to red, but it was a school crossing so she stopped. It was an interminable wait for the green light. Her gaze kept darting impatiently to the light meant for the crossing traffic. Finally it turned to yellow, which meant only a matter of seconds before her lane of traffic would be receiving the green.

Anticipating the light change, Deborah shifted her bare foot from the brake to the accelerator to get a head start on the traffic around her. The light had just changed as the nose of her small car poked itself into the intersection. She didn't see the car that raced to beat the light. She wasn't aware of any danger until she heard the squeal of car brakes and a blaring horn.

Pure instinct made her wrench the steering wheel to angle away from the sound. As the other car skidded sideways into her door, she raised an arm to ward off the shattering glass of her car window. The impact hurtled her sideways to the passenger seat where her shoes, purse and the report lay. Her car seemed to make a slow spin before coming to a rocking stop in the intersection.

Dazed and only half-sure of what had happened, Deborah sat up. There was a funny smattering of red on her dress and she wondered where it had come from. Then she noticed there was a lot of it on her left arm. It seemed to be oozing out of her skin. The fingers of her right hand touched the warm, wet liquid and came away stained. Blood? She didn't feel any pain.

Car doors began slamming. A stranger stuck his head in the window. "Are you all right, lady?" He saw the blood on her arm and ducked his head out to shout to someone. "This one is hurt, too!"

Too? It was a split second before Deborah realized he was referring to the driver of the other car. It prodded her out of the numbed disassociation with reality. The glass from her broken car window must have cut her arm, but the injury wasn't bothering her so it couldn't be too bad. She transferred her concern to the driver of the other car and tried to open her door.

The same stranger said, "The door is bashed in. You'll have to get out on the other side."

Deborah scooted across the seat to the passenger door. It opened easily at her touch. The items on the seat spilled onto the pavement. Someone helped her to pick them up. She remembered thanking the person and worrying about the blood that had dripped from her arm onto the report.

Looking around, she saw the car that had careened off the side of hers. It had rammed into the front of a third car stopped at the light. It was the occupants of the third car who were hurt, not the driver who had run the stoplight. She could hear the distant moans of pain. They were almost instantly drowned out by the wail of police sirens, followed by an ambulance.

When they arrived on the scene, Deborah was caught up in a rush of confusion. Everyone was talking at once, the police asking questions and everyone, including her, answering them. An ambulance attendant was administering first aid to stem the flow of blood from the cut in her arm, and making his own inquiries. The intersection was blocked and horns were blaring with impatience. Policemen were blowing their whistles and directing traffic to a limited degree.

The next thing Deborah knew, she was being ushered into an ambulance and a policeman was handing her shoes, purse, and report to her. One of the more seriously injured victims was being slid into the ambulance on a stretcher.

As the rear doors closed, Deborah heard herself ask, "What time is it?"

"A little after eight, miss," an attendant replied.

She glanced at the report on her lap and remembered, "I have to get to the office. I'm late for work."

"You are going to be later yet," he smiled sympathetically. "That cut needs to be looked at. Your boss will understand."

"You don't know my boss," Deborah murmured. She could just imagine Zane Wilding's reaction to the accident. He would probably accuse her of being an incompetent driver.

At the hospital one of the ambulance attendants ushered her through the emergency entrance while the other two brought in the second victim. Inside, an admitting nurse guided her to one of the treatment rooms where Deborah was subjected to more questions, this time about her medical history, allergies, medication, et cetera. Her answers were jotted down on an admittance form.

"The doctor will be in directly." The nurse started to leave the small cubicle.

"Excuse me, but I'm late for work. How long will it be?" Deborah wanted to know. "There is a nine o'clock meeting and my boss needs that report." At the present moment it was sitting on a straight-backed chair in the room, along with her purse and shoes.

"I'm sorry, Miss Holland, but I don't know. It won't be long, I promise," the nurse assured her. "I'm positive you'll be able to leave as soon as the doctor examines you and sees to that injury."

"But—" Deborah paused in her protest, searching for the words to convince the nurse of the importance of the papers she had in her possession.

"Why don't I call your office and explain the reason for your delay?" the nurse suggested helpfully.

"Yes. My employer is Mr. Wilding, Zane Wilding." She felt slightly relieved by the offer. "He'll probably want to send someone over for these reports rather than wait."

"I'll call him right away," the nurse promised and left.

The minutes dragged while Deborah waited for the doctor to appear. The shock had worn off and her arm had begun to throb. She was sitting on the treatment table, her nylon-stockinged feet dangling over the edge, when she realized she still hadn't put on her shoes. Just as she slid off the table to remedy that, the doctor entered the room along with a nurse.

"Don't tell me my patient is planning to run away," he joked with a pleasant smile.

"I was just going to put on my shoes. I was in such a rush when I left for work this morning, I forgot," Deborah explained, feeling slightly ridiculous as she did.

"I wouldn't bother with them now—" he consulted the chart the nurse handed him before he added "—Miss Holland. Have a seat while I take a look at your arm." He motioned toward the treatment table.

Favoring her left arm, Deborah inched her way onto the table again with as much grace as possible. The doctor unwrapped the temporary bandage that had been applied at the scene of the accident. Blood from the wound had already begun to dry on her skin.

"Messy, isn't it?" he grinned. "But I'll bet it isn't as bad as it looks." No comment seemed to be expected from Deborah and she made none.

The nurse brought him some towelettes and a bowl filled with some solution. Deborah watched as he began cleaning the excess blood from her skin. There were several small cuts, but only one major laceration on the inside of her arm. The flow of blood had been reduced to a slow seepage.

"It's going to require a few stitches," he informed her. "First, we'd better make sure there aren't any glass splinters in there."

Working with professional efficiency, he probed the cut. Deborah winced several times, biting at her lower lip to check the gasps of pain. When the stitching was all done and the injury once again bandaged, the doctor leaned back.

"Any other aches or pains I can treat?" he asked in a half-joking manner. "You didn't hit your head, twist your back?"

"No. Nothing." Deborah shook her had. The movement started a shower of tiny slivers of glass that had been caught in her thick hair.

"You were lucky. You know that, don't you?" the doctor remarked. "If you hadn't lifted your arm, that broken glass would have cut your face more than it did." Glancing at the nurse, he ordered, "Bring me that bowl of antiseptic."

"My face?" She was suddenly conscious of a vague stinging sensation along her left cheek.

"Don't worry," he smiled. "It's just a few tiny nicks. The skin has barely been pricked. They'll be all gone in a couple of days."

His gentle, capable hands swabbed the pinpoints on her cheek. "How is the driver of the third car?" she asked.

"A broken leg, I understand," the nurse was the one who answered her question.

As the doctor finished, a movement in the doorway drew Deborah's gaze. "Zane," she breathed in astonishment, unaware she had used his given name. He entered the treatment room, making it seem smaller than it already was. Something flickered in his shattering blue eyes, but the glimpse was too fleeting for Deborah to identify it.

"Are you a relative?" the doctor was asking in his pleasant voice.

"No, I'm her employer."

"This is Mr. Wilding, doctor." Deborah would have introduced them but she couldn't remember the doctor's name or whether he had told her. Her initial shock at seeing Zane was receding, but her confusion hadn't. "What are you doing here?"

"The hospital called to inform me of your accident."

If he had intended to say more than that, Deborah didn't give him a chance. "Of course, the meeting," she remembered. "Is it nine o'clock yet? The report is on that chair behind you. The first pages are a little smeared with blood. They should be retyped, but—"

"Her face, will it be scarred?" Even as Zane asked the question, interrupting her hastily prepared speech, his strong fingers were closing on her chin and turning her head so he could examine the left side of her face for himself.

His touch stopped her heartbeat before it went racing off on a snare-drum roll. One of his fingers was on the pulse in her neck and Deborah wondered if he had felt her reaction to the unexpected contact. It made her feel hot and slightly giddy.

"No. Those little cuts will go away in a day or two," the doctor assured him. "She did have a bad laceration on her left arm, but we've stitched that up. It'll give her pain for a few days, but I'm sure it will heal perfectly. She will have a scar from that."

A nerve twitched in his hard, lean jaw as his hand fell away from her chin. Deborah had trouble trying to breathe normally again. Zane appeared upset about something. If it wasn't because she was late for work, then she didn't know why.

"Is she free to leave now?" he demanded of the doctor.

"Yes. Here is a couple of prescriptions, one for an antibiotic to ward off any possible infection and the other is for a mild painkiller if it's needed." The doctor rose from his stool after handing two slips of paper to Zane, and smiled at Deborah. "Take care of yourself, Miss Holland. Stop by the desk on your way out and the nurse will give you an appointment to have the stitches removed."

"Thank you." She returned his smile.

"Are these your things?" Zane turned to the chair behind him as the doctor and nurse left the treatment room.

"Yes." His curtness and the grimness of his expression confused Deborah. "The accident wasn't my fault," she asserted just in case an accusation was forthcoming. "The other driver ran a red—"

"Yes, I know," he interrupted, picking up her shoes. "I've already received a full report from the police."

She reached to take her shoes from him, but he was already bending to slip them onto her feet. "I'll do that," she protested in a surge of self-consciousness. But a hand was already cupping her heel and sliding her foot into a shoe. The contact was oddly intimate, not at all resembling the impersonal touch of a shoe salesman.

"You are hardly Cinderella," he remarked in a dry, flat voice.

It prodded her retort. "And you are certainly no Prince Charming."

As he straightened, a cold, crooked smile slanted his mouth. "Now that sounds like you, Miss Holland."

Before she could guess his intentions, his hands were spanning the sides of her rib cage to lift her off the table, setting her feet on the floor. A crazy weakness attacked her legs. Deborah wavered un-

steadily against him for an instant, aware of his hard
strength and an elusive, masculine scent that clung to
his skin. Then he was stepping away, blue eyes revealing nothing of this thoughts. Was it her imagination or
had he held her a fraction of a second longer than
was necessary? And why was she disappointed that
his hands were no longer against her flesh?

Deborah gave herself a mental shake. This was all
insane. Where were these silly, romantic notions
coming from? Zane Wilding was a married man. She
didn't want to become tangled in that kind of
nowhere situation. Plus, despite his rugged good
looks, she didn't like him as a person. He was too
hard and insensitive, totally lacking in compassion
and gentleness. Deborah decided that the accident
had simply knocked her a little more off balance than
she had realized.

"If you are ready, we'll get you signed out of
here." He handed the purse to her, but kept the
report in his possession.

Assured that she had recovered her poise, Deborah
nodded. "Yes, I'm ready." She took the purse he
held out to her.

After they had made the appointment, Zane took
charge of the details of her discharge, accomplishing
the whole procedure at the cashier's desk in record
time. Deborah recognized that his forceful personal-
ity was one few people would argue with and the girl
behind the desk was no exception.

"My car is parked outside."

"What about my car?" Deborah remembered with
a start, stopping halfway to the exit door.

His hand gripped her elbow to propel her forward.

"It's been towed to a garage for repairs. Tom has already handled the details so you don't need to be concerned about it." He pushed the door open and held it for her.

"But—" Deborah felt compelled to assert herself "—it's my car. I have to notify my insurance company and—"

"I told you that it has already been done."

Deborah walked toward the sleek, cobalt blue Continental. She would have stopped without the hand on her elbow. Instead of feeling relieved by his announcement, she felt confused and suspicious.

"But why did you do it?" she demanded. "It wasn't any of your business."

"On the contrary—" Zane unlocked the passenger side and helped her into the seat "—the fact that you work for me, made it my business. We all help in time of necessity. It's called teamwork."

"And you call the shots." But he closed the door on her faintly sarcastic response and Deborah doubted that he had heard her.

It was an unusual experience to have Zane behind the wheel. Usually she or Tom drove, depending on which of them Zane wanted to confer with at the time. But there was no mistaking that the hands on the steering wheel were very strong, very competent, and very much in control—just like the man.

During the first few minutes of the drive, Deborah studied the rawly masculine profile of the driver, the rakish thickness of his jet black hair, and the steel blue of his eyes. Her arm began to throb, distracting her attention. She shifted its position on her lap to relieve the stress of the previous one. Her glance noticed the report on the seat between them.

"What time is it?" she asked suddenly.

"Where is your watch?" His quick glance noticed the bareness of her left wrist.

"I left it on the dresser this morning." In her haste to leave for the office, she had forgotten all about it.

"It's a few minutes before nine."

"The meeting! We'll be late," Deborah realized in a voice that revealed her own feelings of guilt and frustration. "You haven't had a chance to go over the report. The first few pages really should be retyped. I don't suppose there will be time—"

"The meeting has been postponed."

"That's a relief." Deborah relaxed against the plushly upholstered seat of gray velour, and released a sigh that quivered through her nerves, easing their tautness.

"How is your arm?" With a sliding look that was both sharp and impersonal, his gaze ran over the bandage before slicing back to the traffic.

Something clicked in her mind. Deborah had been puzzling over his presence. His show of concern was for totally selfish reasons. How severely was she going to be incapacitated by her injury? How much would it interfere with her ability to do her job? Anger splintered through her.

"Don't worry, Mr. Wilding." Her voice reeked with sarcasm. "It is my left arm. Since I'm right-handed, I'm still able to take notes and function quite capably at the meeting."

"You aren't attending the meeting. I'm taking you to your apartment," Zane announced.

She flashed him a surprised and wary look. "It

isn't necessary. I'm able to work and I know how important this meeting is."

His sharp gaze caught and held hers at a stoplight. "I can manage quite well without you. Contrary to your opinion, your services as my assistant are not indispensable."

Stung by his caustic dismissal of the need for her presence, Deborah faced the front, her pride just a little bit hurt. "I never suggested that they were." *Maybe a little.* Everyone likes to be needed and Deborah wasn't an exception. She liked to think that her contribution was important, but Zane Wilding made it clear that such a belief was a fallacy.

"My God, I suppose your feelings are hurt," he muttered in an impatient undertone and shot her a glittering look. "I was merely trying to point out that we can survive without your presence today. The accident was a traumatic experience, not counting the injury to your arm. I'm offering you a day off—with pay."

Obviously he thought he was doing her a favor. How much more receptive she would have been if he had only said, "Somehow we'll make it through today without you," or at least implied she would be missed. But Zane Wilding never needed anybody, she remembered.

"Thank you." She ground out the polite phrase through gritted teeth and lapsed into a tense silence that didn't end until he had parked in front of her apartment. When he started to get out of the car, Deborah objected, "There isn't any need for you to walk me to the door. I can manage without your help."

There was a split second's hesitation before he shrugged and remained behind the wheel while she stepped onto the sidewalk. The car remained parked at the curb. The skin at the back of her neck prickled as Deborah walked up the flight of stairs to her apartment door. He was watching her, waiting to see that she made it inside. She fumbled in her purse for the key and finally managed to unlock the door, but she didn't reveal her awareness of the car as it pulled away from the curb.

When the door was closed behind her, Deborah was overwhelmed by a feeling of release. She trembled violently and blamed it on the after shock of the accident. Dropping her purse on the sofa, she noticed the red stains on her dress. If she intended to get them out, she had to do something about them right away. Unbelting her dress, Deborah walked into the bathroom and paused at the sight of her reflection in the mirror.

No wonder Zane hadn't thought her capable of a day's work. Her mahogany hair was rumpled without any semblance of style or order. She didn't look the picture of smooth efficiency. A haunting brilliance of pain was in her gray eyes, lacing their usual confident glow of self-possession. Turning her head sideways, Deborah examined the nicks on her cheek, marks that were barely discernible even now.

With vivid clarity, she remembered Zane's sharp inquiry whether her face would be scarred. The firm clasp of his fingers seemed to have left their sensual imprint on her chin. She could still feel them. Why would he care if she had been left with facial scars from the accident? She had worked for him nearly six months, but he was still very much a mystery to her in many ways. Deborah shook her head. Where was it written that she had to know everything there was to know about the man who signed her paycheck?

She stripped off her dress, taking care not to jar her injured arm, and washed out the blood stains with cold water. Wearing just her underclothes, she walked into the bedroom, feeling enervated and tired by all that had happened. She slipped between the covers of the unmade bed and rested her head on the pillow to doze.

At midafternoon, Deborah wakened to the throbbing pain in her arm. It made her restless and on edge. Donning a cotton duster, she ventured into the kitchen. She knew she should eat, but the cold sandwich she fixed tasted like cotton in her mouth. Cradling her left arm in her lap, she tried to read, but the paperback tale didn't hold her interest. She began prowling the room, holding her throbbing left arm against her stomach. It was a long time since she had so much free time to kill. There was a great deal of housework that needed to be done, but the way her arm felt, such activity would only aggravate her discomfort.

She was fixing a glass of iced tea when the doorbell rang. The sound startled her. It was barely five o'clock, not the hour when any of her friends might stop by to see her. She was so infrequently home lately that most of them had stopped calling. But Deborah had been so busy it hadn't mattered. A puzzled frown clouded her expression as she crossed the room to open the door.

"Tom!" She blinked in surprise at the brown-haired man standing on her threshold. "I didn't expect to see you. What are you doing here?" Remembering her manners, she opened the door wider. "Come in."

"I stopped by to see how you are." He walked into the apartment, mild brown eyes smiling at her.

"I'm fine...considering," Deborah qualified the statement with an offhand shrug. "I'm glad you came by. I was just pouring myself a glass of iced tea. Would you like some?"

"Sounds good." As she walked to the kitchen counter, he glanced around the modern studio apartment. "You have a nice place."

"Thank you." She handed him a glass of tea and turned to retrieve her own.

Tom noticed the way she cradled her left arm in front of her to relieve the pressure. "How's that arm?" He sipped at his tea, studying her over the rim of his glass.

"It aches." It felt as if it were swollen twice its size, which of course it wasn't.

"Have you taken the pain pills the doctor prescribed for you?" He must have guessed that she was understating her discomfort, because his brown eyes narrowed in quiet speculation.

"No."

"Why?"

"Because I don't believe in taking pills. The body should feel pain when it's hurt," Deborah answered defensively. The telephone rang and staved off the argument forming on Tom's lips. Setting the glass of tea on the counter, she lifted the receiver of the wall phone. "Holland residence."

"Deborah?"

The rich timbre of Zane Wilding's voice vibrated through her. Her heart skittered across her rib cage to create a funny sensation in the pit of her stomach. The way he said her name made it sound different, not quite belonging to her. Coming from him, it was always Miss Holland. There was something decidedly intimate in the use of her first name. It strangled her throat.

"Yes." Deborah forced the word out after a breathlessly long pause.

"Has Tom arrived yet?"

She darted a look at the man in question. "Yes."

"Let me speak to him."

She couldn't acknowledge the order. Instead she shoved the receiver toward Tom and announced tightly, "It's for you."

As he took the telephone from her, Deborah grabbed for her iced-tea glass, needing something in her hands to hide her trembling. Zane could have at least asked how she was, she thought bitterly and realized she was feeling sorry for herself.

Her back was to Tom, but she heard him say, "Her color is good but she says her arm is hurting her. It goes against her principles to take the pain pills the doctor prescribed. . .I'll tell her," Tom said in response to whatever Zane had said.

The statement made Deborah turn around, curious to know what message he was supposed to relay to her. After that Tom's responses became monosyllabic. Yet the way he kept looking at her gave Deborah the impression the conversation was still focused on her.

When Tom hung up the telephone, Deborah attempted a nonchaleant inquiry. "What was that all about?"

"Zane said he didn't care what your principles were. You are supposed to take one of those pain pills. As a matter of fact, he made it a direct order," Tom smiled in a bemused way.

"Because it's a direct order from him, that's supposed to make a difference?" she mocked.

"Because it's a direct order, you are supposed to do what you always do—obey it without question," he replied half in jest and half seriously. "Honestly, Deborah, it will help you rest and relax."

"Perhaps." She abandoned her ice-tea glass and hugged her right arm protectively over her left. Bitterness crept into her voice. "But don't pretend that *he* cares how I feel."

"If you had seen him after he received that telephone call from the hospital this morning, you wouldn't say that. Zane was upset," he insisted gently.

"Sure, he was upset," she agreed acidly. "The accident forced a postponement of his business meeting. He had to find out whether he was going to be forced to find someone to take my place. I'm not indispensable, Tom. He made that quite clear."

"None of us is indispensable—not even Zane. I think you took whatever he said too personally."

"If I did, I certainly can't blame him, can I?" Deborah laughed and it was a derisive sound. "Nothing with him is ever personal. He must be the original iceman—with all his feelings frozen inside."

Tom swirled the liquid in his glass and watched the tiny whirlpool of brown tea. "These last few years

Zane has suppressed nearly all of his emotions to lead a monklike existence. It has made him appear hard and without feeling. Don't be taken in by the facade, Deborah. He cares, but he's blocked all the outlets that might let it show."

Her head was tipped to the side in an attitude that was both skeptical and intrigued. "Monklike existence" was the last phrase she would have attributed to Zane. There was so much raw virility about him that it defied the imagination to conceive of his taking a vow of celibacy.

"Are you trying to tell me that—" Deborah began in scoffing amusement.

But Tom interrupted, crossing the room to the sofa. "I don't have to tell you about his marriage. I'm sure your imagination is vivid enough. But when Zane took the vows 'for better or worse, in sickness and in health,' he meant them."

His words led Deborah into a mental maze, a labyrinth of thoughts that didn't offer a quick escape. She was conscious of Tom picking up her purse and exploring its contents, but it didn't really register in her mind. He crossed the room to stand in front of her.

"Open your mouth," he ordered. When she did, he placed a white pill on her tongue and handed her the glass of iced tea from the counter. "Drink."

She washed the pill down without realizing what she was doing. Tom had shown her a new facet to her employer's character. And Deborah wasn't sure it was one she wanted to explore.

"Will you feel like coming to work in the morning?" Tom asked.

"Yes. I'd rather be working than sitting around here." Her reply was absent but truthful.

"Your car won't be fixed until Monday, so I'll pick you up in the morning. Around eight?"

"That's late."

"So? Enjoy the pampering and stop complaining," he teased.

Deborah smiled, as he intended her to do. "Eight o'clock and I wasn't complaining."

"Have you eaten?"

"A sandwich."

He grimaced at that. Her opinion precisely. "There's a great seafood place down the street. Why don't I go bring us back something to eat?"

"Sounds great." Much better than trying to eat alone.

It was eight o'clock that evening before Tom finally left. It had been a very enjoyable evening, too. Tom was easy to talk to, and a witty conversationalist, as well. Not one word of business had been spoken, which was definitely a novelty. The pain in her arm had been reduced to a dull ache by the time Deborah crawled into bed shortly after he'd left. She immediately fell asleep.

CHAPTER FIVE

TOM WAS SITTING on the corner of her desk, in the middle of telling a joke. "This fire-and-brimstone preacher finishes his sermon with a cry that all the liquor in every house should be taken to the river and emptied into it. Then he gives a baleful look at the congregation and gives them instructions to rise and open their hymnbooks to number 201—"

Deborah anticipated the punch line and began singing, "Shall We Gather at the River." They both broke into laughter.

"You've heard it before," he accused.

"No, honestly," she denied. "It was just so obvious."

"It was, wasn't it?" he agreed and they laughed again.

At the sound of the door opening, Deborah glanced up to see Zane walk in. It was almost two weeks since the accident and her arm had healed nicely. The only lingering aftereffect from the incident was the funny, curling sensation in the pit of her stomach when her employer appeared without prior warning. It was happening now. His impassive expression wiped the smile from her face.

"I hope the two of you have accomplished some

serious work in my absence," he remarked in a searingly dry tone.

Tom turned, smiling easily. "Hello, Zane. I was just telling Deborah a joke I'd heard," he was explaining their laughter but not defending it.

The explanation didn't soften his expression as Zane stopped at her desk. "When you are sufficiently recovered to attend to serious business, bring me the geological study on the Sand-Sea project."

His attitude riled Deborah's temper. As he turned away from her desk, she muttered, "I don't know where you lost your sense of humor, Mr. Wilding, but I wish you'd find it."

He paused, half turning to give her a sidelong look of lazy challenge. "Would you like to suggest a place where I might look for it, Miss Holland?"

She had expected him to ignore her comment. For an instant, she hesitated. He was her employer, but a little voice goaded her with the reminder that he had asked for a suggestion. She lifted her chin a fraction of an inch to meet his gaze.

"Yes, I would." Deborah smiled with taunting sweetness. "Why don't you go to hell to find it?"

"I have a busy schedule. It's your job to fit these little side trips in, Miss Holland." It was impossible, but there seemed to be a glint of amusement in those usually cold blue eyes.

Tom laughed, knowing her remark had been successfully countered. "What now, Deborah?"

A suitable retort escaped her, but Zane negated the need for one by speaking first. "Now she can bring me that study. We have a lot of business to get out of the way before I leave for California, so be prepared for a long day." With the warning issued, Zane walked to his desk to begin work.

"No rest for the wicked," Tom sighed mockingly and straightened from her desk. "You know where to find me if you need me."

Deborah gave him an answering nod but didn't verbally respond. His office was hidden away in the accounting section. Over the months, Deborah had learned that Tom Brookshire was something of a mathematical whiz, an expert in accounting and computers as well as a fairly accurate economic forecaster. Plus he held a law degree, although numbers were his particular fascination.

As Tom left, closing the door, Deborah sifted through the stacks of papers, reports and notes piled on her desk. She never seemed to make any headway when it came to clearing it, only in shifting the papers from one stack to another. For all the disorganized appearance of her desk top, there was a system to it. She found the geological survey report almost immediately and carried it to his desk.

Zane barely looked up when she set it in front of him. "Get Dan Adams on the phone for me, Deborah."

Her heart did a little flip. He had used her name unconsciously, influenced by Tom's ready use of it. It had happened a half dozen times since the accident, usually when it was just the two of them in the office. Coming at unexpected times, like now, it did funny things to her, ruffling her composure and throwing her momentarily off balance.

Deborah nodded an affirmative response to his request. Since Zane wasn't looking at her, he didn't see it. "Was there anything else, Mr. Wilding?" she asked, her voice sounding quite controlled and businesslike.

This close, she caught the lingering scent of chlorine that the soap hadn't washed away after his noon-hour swim in the pool. Deborah had never taken him up on his offer to indulge in an hour of exercise and sun on her lunch break. But there were times when she envied his invigorated glow after one of those sessions.

Zane didn't immediately respond to her question, finishing the note he was jotting on a margin of a report. He combed his fingers through his black hair that gleamed with the texture of rumpled silk, before lifting his head.

"Have you finished transcribing those notes on the environmental impact study?" he questioned with an absent frown.

"Mrs. Haines is typing them now."

"I want to see them as soon as she's done." It was a dismissal and Deborah returned to her desk.

THE STREETLIGHTS CAME ON outside the window, signaling the darkness of the hour. Deborah was seated in a straight chair in front of Zane's desk, taking down his rapid dictation. True to his prediction, it was turning out to be a marathon day. Tom had stuck his head in twenty minutes ago to say if there was nothing more, he was leaving. Zane had waved a dismissal with barely a pause.

The rumblings of her empty stomach were growing louder. Surely, Deborah thought, he could hear them and get the message. Her fingers ached from gripping the pencil so tightly to keep up with his rapid pace. Her concentration was wavering after the long hours she had already put in. Deborah found herself unable to keep with with him.

"Slow down a minute," she complained. He paused until her pencil stopped its scratching on her steno pad, then started again.

He had barely got the next sentence out when the door burst open. "I knew I'd find the two of you together!" a hysterical voice screamed in accusation.

"Sylvia!" Zane was on his feet, glaring angrily at the wild-eyed blonde weaving into the room, before Deborah had even turned around.

"Don't sound so outraged!" his wife mocked in a slurring voice. "I've finally caught you. Don't think for one minute I'm taken in by the supposed innocence of this scene. I know you've been making love to her. But you heard me coming and—"

"That's enough, Sylvia!" His voice was an explosion of anger that made Deborah cringe involuntarily, an automatic reaction to a violent noise.

But Sylvia Wilding must have been too numbed by alcohol to feel the reverberating shock waves of his anger. "You can't fool me!" she screamed in a nearly demented voice. "Just look at her face." She waved a limp hand toward Deborah. "She isn't as good at controlling her emotions as you are. Her face is red as a beet."

It was true. Deborah could feel the scarlet heat staining her cheeks, but not for the reason his wife was implying. Not because it was true, but because of the disturbing picture her mind had just painted of her locked in a passionate embrace with her employer.

"If Miss Holland is embarrassed, it's because she would prefer not to witness you making a fool of yourself with your absurd accusations," Zane snapped.

"Absurd!" his wife began.

"Yes, absurd! Open your eyes, Sylvia, if you can see through that alcoholic haze," he added contemptuously. "Does it really look as if I've been chasing Miss Holland around my desk? Are either of us out of breath? Are our clothes mussed?"

His wife looked from one to the other. She seemed to crumple before Deborah's very eyes into a sobbing, tragically pathetic creature.

"You may leave, Miss Holland," Zane issued the stiff order. When Deborah didn't immediately move to obey, he added a strident, *"Now!"*

Normally she would have made an attempt at straightening her cluttered desk, but this time Deborah just set her steno pad and pencil on top of some papers and grabbed her purse from a bottom drawer.

All the while Sylvia Wilding kept sobbing over and over again. "I'm sorry, Zane. Forgive me. Please, forgive me."

But as Deborah walked out of the office, he had made no move to comfort the crying woman. He was still standing rigidly behind his desk. Deborah felt that old surge of resentment at his callousness and slammed the door. He had about as much compassion as one of his computers.

Halfway down the corridor to the exit, Deborah

realized that she didn't have her car keys. They were lying on her desk in the office where she'd left them that morning. She'd have to go back for them. It couldn't be helped.

Reentering the outer office, she crossed the darkened room to the door of Zane Wilding's private office. As she turned the knob to enter, she heard the voices inside and hesitated. Sylvia's crying had been reduced to occasional hiccuping sounds.

"I need a drink, Zane." She sounded frantic. "Don't you have any whiskey in this place?" There were noises that suggested she was searching the desks and cabinets for liquor.

"You aren't going to find Ethan in any bottle." His voice was like a whip, slashing and cutting, more destroying than if he had shouted. "If you keep drinking, it will kill you."

"But don't you see—that's what I want! I want to die!" His wife cried. "I want to be with my son again! I want to be with Ethan!"

"You don't know what you're saying. Come on. I'm taking you home." The fury in his harsh tone was severely checked.

Deborah hovered indecisively. Should she make her presence known or would it be better to wait in the shadows until they had left? She backed a step away from the door, nibbling at her lip as she tried to decide.

"Don't touch me!" Sylvia screamed. "I can't stand it!"

There was a crash and the sound of glass breaking. An eerie cry of terror sent shivers down Deborah's spine. From inside the room, she heard Zane's muffled curse.

"Dammit, Sylvia. Look what you've done!" he muttered savagely.

"It hurts, Zane," his wife whimpered.

"I'm surprised you can feel anything." His dry retort was particularly cutting.

Overwhelmed by curiosity, Deborah couldn't stand to remain outside not knowing what had happened. She didn't care whether her presence was wanted or not. She opened the door and stopped just inside the room. Zane was wrapping a handkerchief around his wife's hand, the white linen showing the red stains of blood. Sylvia was watching with almost hypnotized horror.

His blue gaze slashed to Deborah, pinning her where she stood. "What are you doing here?"

"I left my car keys on the desk. What happened?" She stared at him with vague accusation in her gray eyes. In her mind, she blamed Zane indirectly for whatever had happened. If he hadn't treated his wife so roughly, she wouldn't have become so hysterical.

"My wife cut her hand on some broken glass. It isn't serious." He finished wrapping the handkerchief and attempted to put an arm around his wife's shoulders. "I'll take you home."

But she cringed away from him. "No."

His impatience was almost tangible. "Help me get my wife to the car, Miss Holland."

It was a request she could hardly refuse since his wife was making it so obvious that she wouldn't let him near her. Slinging her purse over her shoulder,

Deborah walked forward to speak to the woman calmly.

"Why don't you come with me, Mrs. Wilding?" she suggested. "We'll take care of that hand."

A glazed pair of eyes blinked at her with the innocence of a baby. "A drink," she asked in a small voice. "I need a drink, too. Can I have one?"

"Later, after we've bandaged your hand." Maybe it wasn't fair to make a promise like that, but Deborah didn't care. At the moment it seemed no different from promising candy to a child, although she knew it was. "Come along now."

She curved an arm around the blonde's shoulders and Sylvia didn't resist, but meekly let herself be guided toward the door. The unsteadiness of her legs made the woman lean heavily against Deborah. Her breath reeked of whiskey. It was so potent it almost gagged Deborah. Zane walked ahead of them to open the doors.

At the car, he unlocked a rear side door. Deborah had to almost physically lift his wife onto the rear passenger seat. Sylvia roused from her stupor long enough to look around her and take stock of the surroundings.

"Where are you taking me? What's happening?" The forlorn thread of her voice sounded frightened and lost.

"Ssh," Deborah soothed and slid into the seat beside her. She couldn't abandon Sylvia to Zane's questionable care. "It's all right. We're just going someplace to take care of your hand."

Reassured, the blonde cuddled up to her like a baby seeking the comfort of her mother's arms.

Deborah rocked her, aware of the clenched fists of the man standing beside the car, but she didn't acknowledge his presence with a look. The closing of the door was followed by the opening of the driver's door as Zane slid behind the wheel.

Not a word was exchanged between Deborah and Zane during the short drive to his city condominium. Out of Sylvia's unintelligible ramblings, Deborah was able to understand only a word or two here and there... *my baby, Ethan*, and *a drink*. The woman had obviously never recovered from the grief of losing her only child. It was a grief she should have shared with her husband, but considering who her husband was, Deborah understood why Sylvia was shouldering it alone, and why she had broken under the strain. She glared her condemnation at the insensitive brute behind the wheel.

When the car was parked, Deborah tried to rouse the woman in her arms, without success. The interior light flared as Zane opened the rear door. The blonde was a deadweight, her mouth open and her eyes closed.

"Wake up, Mrs. Wilding. We're here." Deborah shook her gently.

"Leave her be. She's out cold." Zane didn't make any attempt to keep the sharp impatience out of his tone. "Move out of the way and I'll carry her in."

Disentangling herself from the woman's arms, Deborah slid out of the passenger seat, lying the woman down carefully as she did. She moved out of the way to stand on the sidewalk while Zane reached into the backseat to drag his wife's limp body out. He shifted her petite form into the cradle he'd made with his arms, and kicked the car door shut. Although Sylvia was a small woman, her lifeless state had to have added pounds to her weight. But Zane strode up the sidewalk as if she weighed no more than a child. Deborah followed him, since it seemed the logical thing to do.

Zane paused beneath a lighted doorway and pushed a buzzer. Within seconds, the summons was answered by a gray-haired woman in a black dress that resembled a uniform. His housekeeper, Deborah guessed. The gray-haired woman took one look at the blonde in his arms and immediately swung the door wide to admit them.

"Madelaine called. I'll phone her back and tell her Sylvia is here," the housekeeper stated.

There was an acknowledging nod from Zane. While the housekeeper scurried off into one of the rooms and closed the door, Zane carried his wife across the short entryway and up a flight of stairs. Deborah hesitated at the base of the stairs, wondering if she should go up to help. At that moment, the housekeeper came bustling past her to climb the stairs. Obviously she wouldn't be needed, so Deborah waited below.

After nearly twenty minutes, she was just about convinced they had forgotten she was down there waiting. Her stomach began growling hungrily again, which only increased her irritation. Someone could have at least offered her a cup of coffee. A footstep on the stairs spun her around. The housekeeper descended, her relatively unlined face an impassive mask that rivaled her employer's ability to conceal his thoughts.

"I have phoned for a taxi. A cab is on its way to take you home," she informed Deborah.

Deborah stared at her wordlessly until she realized that she wasn't going to receive any thank you or any expression of appreciation for her help in getting Mrs. Wilding home. She wasn't even going to be told how the woman was.

"I'll wait for it outside!" she snapped and pivoted to cross the entryway to the door.

She was boiling mad at the way she had been treated, and the coolness of the night air had no effect on her raging anger. Stalking like a caged tigress, she paced back and forth on a small square of sidewalk in front of the condominium. A few minutes later, a taxi pulled up in front. Deborah didn't wait for the driver to get out to open the passenger door, but climbed into the back unaided. She gave him the address of the office building and began rummaging through her purse for a cigarette. The pack was empty when she finally found it.

"Excuse me." She leaned forward to tap the driver on the shoulder. "Do you have a cigarette? I'm out and I could use one right now."

"Sure." He handed her back a pack of filtered cigarettes so she could help herself. He glanced in the rearview mirror and watched the jerky, agitated movements as she lighted the cigarette. "Did you have a fight with your fella?"

"No." She exhaled an irritated stream of smoke. "My boss."

"What's the matter? Doesn't he pay you overtime?"

"Oh, he pays." Her voice was husky from her

effort to contain the anger bubbling inside. "He just forgets to say thanks."

"I know the feeling, lady," the cab driver commiserated, and made no further attempt to continue the conversation.

When they stopped in front of the office building, Deborah leaned forward to pay him. "The fare has already been taken care of...and I'll add a generous tip for myself," he winked and climbed out to open her door. "Don't work too hard."

"I won't." She gave him a tense, absent smile as she stepped out of the cab.

Her car keys were still on her desk in the office. Pausing beneath a streetlight, Deborah searched her purse for the office keys to get into the locked building. She found them immediately and hurried up the sidewalk to the front entrance. Inside, her footsteps echoed hollowly through the empty corridor.

When she reached the private office, Deborah stopped inside the door to turn the light switch on. She started to cross over to her desk, but her glance strayed to the play of light on the broken pieces of glass scattered on the carpet. Since she was there, she decided that she might as well clean it up rather than leave it until morning.

Setting her purse aside, she walked over to Zane's desk and bent down to pick up the fragmentary remains of the crystal vase. Deborah started with the bigger chips, taking care not to cut her own hand on the sharp edges. The wastebasket stood in a corner. She emptied a handful of glass into it, then carried the basket over to where the rest of the broken glass lay. The crystal fragments made a faint ringing sound as she tossed them into the metal container.

The sound of the door opening startled her. Deborah straightened to whirl around, not certain whether she expected to confront a security guard or an intruder. But she certainly hadn't expected to receive the rapier thrust of Zane's piercing look.

"What the hell are you doing here, Miss Holland? How many times do I have to send you home before you get the message?" he snapped.

Of all the ungrateful, arrogant—Deborah closed her mind to all the adjectives she could have used to describe him. "I stopped to get my car keys and decided to clean up this mess." Her temper simmered to a quick boil. "And thank you very much, Miss Holland, for helping me with my wife. It was so thoughtful and considerate of you to ride with her," she mocked him with all the simple words of gratitude he should have said. "I hope it wasn't too much trouble. You must be tired after the long day at work, Miss Holland. Why don't you go home and get some rest?" Deborah paused to take a breath and change to a sweetly demure voice. "I will do that, Mr. Wilding. In fact, I'll be leaving in just a few minutes."

He waited in grim silence as if expecting her tirade to continue.

"Are you through?" he challenged when it didn't.

"Is that all you can say?" she gazed at him in astonishment. Not a thing she had said had struck home. Recognizing that it was hopeless to ever expect him to admit he was wrong, Deborah turned away and answered his question before he could respond to hers. "Yes, I'm through...for the time being anyway." She needed the release of doing something to vent all the violent energy her anger had generated. "But working for you, I'm sure there will be other occasions when I will lose my temper," she finished, tossing the ever smaller crystal fragments into the garbage with a vengeance.

"I may have been remiss in thanking you for your assistance with my wife this evening," Zane began in a hard, tight voice, but he ultimately lost control. "Will you leave that damned glass be, and get off that floor? I'll clean it up myself!"

Deborah half turned but she didn't rise; her gray eyes were blazing. "Please," she prompted.

"What?" A dark frown gathered on his forehead; he was completely at a loss as to her meaning.

"*Please*, leave the glass, and *please* get off the floor." She stressed with forceful emphasis.

"Oh, for God's sake." He turned his head to the side, muttering in exasperation. When he looked back at her, it was to issue a taut, "Please," with an insolence that was about as impolite as a person could get.

For a fleeting second, Deborah wondered if she were trying to teach manners to a jungle panther. The glitter in those blue eyes was decidedly menacing. Straightening, she brushed nervously at her skirt before again meeting his look.

"That's much better." Her smile was tense. "People generally react more favorably when there is a little polite consideration shown. Everyone needs a kind word now and then. Maybe if you had been a little kinder to your wife tonight instead of being so hard with her, she wouldn't have become so hysterical. She needs—"

One second, half the width of the room separated them. In the next, Deborah found that her shoulders were caught in the steel jaws of a trap and she was being yanked against a solid rock wall. The impact ripped the breath from her lungs.

"She needs!" The bronze mask had been removed from his features, revealing an anger that had been bottled up too long. "What about what *I* need? Ethan was my son, too!" A fiery anguish burned in his eyes as they scorched her face, which he had forced close to his. "Where was she when *I* needed her? Why did I have to be strong for both of us while she was protected and sedated from the harsh reality of his death?"

"I didn't know," Deborah whispered. Never once had she considered the depth of his pain, but she saw it in the savage violence of his face, a wounded animal lashing out. His fingers were digging into her soft flesh, hurting her, but she didn't cry out or struggle against his maddened hold. "I'm sorry, Zane." And she meant it.

"It's always *her* needs, but there are things that I want, little things that should be so easy to provide." His low voice took on a different intensity that vibrated through Deborah's system. "A pair of eyes to look into that are clear and bright, instead of glazed by an alcohol stupor."

The blue force of his gaze seemed to weld itself to the gray of her eyes. Deborah was shaken by the impression that he could see deep inside her, all the way to her soul. The brilliance of his look seemed to blind her to all other sensations, including the hands that loosened their grip on her shoulders to glide down her backbone and mold her to his length.

"I want a body against mine that isn't flaccid and limp from too much drink. I want it to be firm and alive." The husky murmurings of his voice seemed to awaken her flesh to the roaming caresses of his hands, exploring her waist, hips, and spine with sensual thoroughness.

She spread her fingers across his chest in mute protest to the reactions that were taking place inside her. The taut, muscled lines of his thighs were pressing against hers, inflaming her skin with their hard masculinity. The heat coursing through her gave Deborah the feeling she was boneless, too weak to withstand this sensuous onslaught. Desires that had lain dormant for so long—in both of them—were being fanned to life.

"And. . . ." Zane paused. Her heartbeat quickened as his gaze lingered on her mouth. "I want to kiss a pair of lips that don't taste like whiskey."

His fingers curled into the sleek bun at the back of her neck, destroying its tidy smoothness. He held her head still, as if he expected resistance, while his mouth descended to claim her lips. He devoured them hungrily, savoring and exploring, plundering their softness. Deborah felt her appetite rising to the fever pitch of his. Common sense screamed its alarm, warning her of the danger in his seduction.

A war waged inside her between the needs of the flesh and the spirit. Zane's overwhelming dominance of her nearly pushed the scales to the physical side, promising a wild, delirious joy. Her mind fought through the heady sensations to argue—after the joy came bitterness. While Zane nibbled at her earlobe, his tongue made its own little forays. Deborah realized this might be her only chance to stop this scene from reaching its climax—if that's what she wanted to do. It wasn't what she wanted, but—

"Am I supposed to fulfill your needs, Zane?" She strangled out the tremors that threatened to make her question weak. Her voice wasn't very strong, but its tone was level. "Is that one of my duties, like making coffee for you in the mornings?"

She felt him grow rigid. It took all her control not to wind her arms around his neck and encourage the embrace. But she knew her decision was the right one, even if it left her empty and aching inside.

Abruptly Zane released her and turned away. Her legs almost refused to function without the virile support of his, but she managed to remain standing. His back was to her, but Deborah could see the harsh rhythm of his breathing as he struggled for control. She wanted to reach out to him, touch him, but she didn't dare. Bending his dark head, he rubbed the back of his neck in a gesture that was weary and a little dispirited.

"You'll have to forgive me for that." There was a trace of hoarseness in his voice that was otherwise level. "I forgot myself for a moment and remembered only that I was a man."

"No, you are just human...like the rest of us," Deborah offered quietly, because she, too, had nearly yielded to the sweet temptation of his arms.

"Good night, Miss Holland." It was an icy dismissal.

But at least he hadn't told her to forget what had happened, Deborah thought as she picked up her purse and walked to the desk for her car keys. It would have been impossible to forget. Leaving the office for the darkness of the rest of the building, Deborah realized that she didn't regret what had happened. She knew now what Zane had been through and recognized the sheer loneliness of his existence without love... without passion. Zane was hard, yes, but he was also very human.

CHAPTER SIX

"I DO LOVE a good polka, don't you?" Foster Darrow declared, his florid face even redder than usual after the fast-stepping dance.

"Yes, I do." Deborah was out of breath and trying hard not to pant, after the unaccustomed demands of that dance. The heat in her face warned her that her cheeks were flushed, too. She could feel tendrils of hair curling damply around her neck, having escaped the coil of mahogany hair atop her head. She was badly in need of a few minutes to catch her breath and freshen up. "Would you excuse me, please?"

"Of course," the financier grinned.

And Deborah angled away from the path that would have taken her to the table where Tom and Zane waited. She didn't care what business discussion went on in her absence. She would have been too exhausted to pay attention anyway.

Tonight's meeting was very important. Foster Darrow would be giving Zane his decision whether he would put the support of his financial institution behind the latest LaCosta project. Most people thought these big money decisions were made in large boardrooms or an attorney's office. That was only where the fine details were worked out. The committing of funds was more often done over a lobster thermidor or a manhattan. It was a lesson Deborah had learned very quickly.

In the luxurious powder room, Deborah sank onto one of the velvet-covered stools in front of the long vanity mirror. Her ribs ached from the bear-hugging arm of the heavyset financier. She reached for a tissue in the decorative holder and pressed it against her skin to absorb the thin film of perspiration that had collected on her forehead, cheeks and neck.

Her hair was a mess, little wisps sticking out all over the place. Sighing, Deborah began pulling out the pins and shaking the deep copper length of her hair free. One more polka and it would happen anyway, she reasoned, so why fight it? She took the small comb from her evening purse and arranged her hair into some semblance of a style.

The few minutes of inactivity had slowed her heartbeat to a more normal rhythm. Deborah freshened her lipstick and leaned back to survey the repaired product. Her mind flashed back to that first dinner with Foster Darrow so many months ago. His wife and daughter had been along that time.

After all these months of talks, dinners, cocktails, and endless negotiations, it was going to be settled tonight. She was nervous about the outcome. Not that it meant the project would fail without Darrow's financial backing. They would have to wine and dine someone else and more time would be lost.

Zane was tense, too. Not that he showed it. But Deborah had gained valuable insight into her employer that night the bronze mask he wore, had broken. She no longer accepted what she saw on the surface, but kept looking for the man. In critical situations, such as tonight, she had discovered that he had a tendency to smile with just one side of his mouth. It was an action that always appeared aloofly mocking—a don't-give-a-damn attitude. She suspected that he really didn't. Zane rolled high for the thrill of gambling. He liked the danger, the excitement and the risks of big business. He had poured his whole life into it, because there was nothing left for him outside of it.

It was a sad fact. He had an empty marriage. Deborah didn't pity him, because he wasn't the kind of man a person would pity. Neither he nor Sylvia was to blame for what had happened. Deborah realized that. From the very little she had gleaned 'from Tom on her first encounter with the unbalanced side of Sylvia Wilding, Zane's wife had never been very emotionally stable. The loss of a child, their only child, had been more than she could take. Not even Zane's strength had been enough to help her through it. That wasn't his fault. It wasn't anybody's fault, which was probably the hardest thing to accept of all.

Zane's poignant declarations of his needs echoed back to her, as they had done many a night since the one when he had whispered them to her a month ago. Deborah remembered how she had mocked Tom's inference of his monklike existence. Zane's murmured yearnings had added confirmation. But his obvious virility was so at odds with vows of celibacy and fidelity, that she had continued to doubt. She was ashamed to admit—even to herself—that she had engaged in some discreet snooping before she was finally convinced.

His personal address book contained no telephone numbers or names that weren't directly related to business or relatives. She had even got her hands on his personal bank statements for the past year. Every source she had checked revealed there weren't any women—either on a permanent or temporary basis.

Deborah gave herself a mental shake. she had promised herself she wouldn't think about his personal life, especially his love life. He was her employer and he was married. . . and that was the end of it. Zane had successfully managed to ignore the incident. He hadn't forgotten it. That was something her woman's instinct knew because there were times he watched her when he didn't think she knew.

Two women entered the powder room chatting noisily. It seemed noisy after the silence of her thoughts. Their intrusion served to remind her that it was time she was returning to the table.

Rising from the stool, she smiled distantly at the two women and left the powder room. Deborah wound her way through the crowded lounge to the table where the three men sat. They didn't see her approach until she was standing beside her chair. Belatedly there was an attempt by all three to stand, but she waved them down.

"With your hair down like that, you look like a girl ready to abandon herself to another polka," Foster Darrow declared jovially.

"It was simpler than trying to fix the other style," Deborah admitted, aware of the gaze from the man next to her inspecting her changed appearance. The look was almost a physical touch, but she did her best to appear oblivious to it. "As for the polka, it will have to wait until I've had a chance to quench my thirst."

"Dancing makes you dry," the financier agreed with a hearty laugh.

"Would you like a soft drink?" Zane leaned forward to make the inquiry. Deborah nearly jumped when she realized his hand was on the back of her chair. The accidental brush of his fingertips against the bare skin of her back sparked an immediate tingling of her flesh.

"No, this is fine," she insisted and reached for the watered-down gin and lime drink.

"Cigarette?" The financier offered her one from his case and lighted it for her. "I'm going to have to have a talk with the men of your generation. You are a beautiful and intelligent woman, Deborah. Some man should have snatched you up and married you a long time ago."

The sun-browned hand had been removed from her chair. Deborah leaned back, striking a pose intended to appear casual and unconcerned.

"I have always had ambitions of my own. I guess I've never met a man who put the thought of marriage in my mind." There was one man who could have, under different circumstances. Her gaze ricocheted to Zane and glanced just as quickly away from his narrowly veiled look. She leaned forward to tap her cigarette in the ashtray.

"Spoken like a true liberated lady," Foster smiled. "Complete unto yourself and not needing the support of a man. You're happy with your life as it stands."

"I wouldn't go so far as to say that." Her natural

honesty wouldn't permit it. "In the mornings when I have to wake up alone and fix my breakfast alone, and sit down at the table alone, that's the time when I'm lonely as hell."

As she spoke, Deborah was studying the burning tip of her cigarette. It was a short distance from it to the face of the man sitting beside her. An inner force compelled her to look his way. She was trapped by a bright blue flame of understanding. It caught at her breath, stealing it from her.

She tried to deny the havoc that searing blue gaze was creating inside, and attempted to · joke, "Of course, since I've worked for Mr. Wilding, I haven't had time to sit around the breakfast table feeling sorry for myself."

There was that crooked smile, that slanted lift of his mouth. "No, you generally wait until you get to the office to have your coffee and a Danish."

"Now you know my secret," Deborah laughed, only there was a tightness in her throat.

"Personally I can't eat when I first get up in the morning," Tom inserted and successfully broke the spell that had locked Deborah's gaze to Zane's. "I always have to wait a couple of hours."

"So do I," Foster agreed. "Now, my wife, she wakes up and immediately eats a gargantuan breakfast. I don't see how she does it."

The conversation digressed into a discussion of eating habits with Foster Darrow and Tom being the main participants. When Deborah crushed out her cigarette in the ashtray, the financier excused himself from the table.

Tom darted her a conspiratorial grin. "Maybe I

should go bribe the band *not* to play another polka."
Like Deborah, he had guessed where Foster Darrow
was going and for what purpose.

"I don't mind," she shrugged in resignation.
"You know what they say—keep 'em happy. That's
my job."

"You were not hired, Miss Holland, to amuse
prospective associates." Zane's voice slashed apart
the lighthearted atmosphere, its low, rumbling tone
ominous in its contained anger. "If you don't wish to
dance with the man, you have only to refuse."

"I didn't mean that literally," she replied, just a
little angry that he thought she was the type that
would let herself be used in that way. "You should
know that I'm capable of saying no to a situation I
don't want."

Unconsciously Deborah had forced him to recall
the night she had rejected his advances. Even in the
dimness of the lounge, she saw him whiten at her
reminder, the flare of his nostrils and the thinning of
his mouth. She had struck a raw nerve that hadn't
healed for either of them, and she regretted her
words.

"And you were right to do so," Zane snapped.

His usage of the past tense caused Deborah to dart
a quick glance at Tom to see if he had caught it.
Foster Darrow chose that moment to return to the
table and Tom had already been distracted by his approach. Deborah couldn't tell if he'd heard Zane's
slip.

As the financier stopped beside her chair, the
dance band struck up a polka tune. "They are playing our song, Deborah," the man joked.

To escape the table and the sudden tension between her and Zane, Deborah placed her hand in the one the financier proffered and rose to dance with him. She even managed a bright smile as she agreed, "So they are, Mr. Darrow."

When the song ended and the financier escorted Deborah back to the table, Zane began to press for a decision. At first, Foster Darrow appeared to resent the injection of business into what had all the earmarks of a social evening, regardless of its actual purpose. Deborah worried that Zane's timing was wrong, but within a short space of time, the financier was enmeshed in the details of the project. He didn't even notice when the band played another polka.

Her concentration wavered and Deborah missed the point in the conversation when Foster responded with an affirmative decision. The next thing she knew Zane was reaching in front of her to shake the financier's hand and clinch the deal. Dazed, it took her a few minutes to realize what had happened.

Elation at their victory was just surfacing as Zane uncoiled his length from the chair. "It's been a long day, Foster. I still haven't adjusted to the change in time zones. I'm sure you'll understand if we call it a night. Tomorrow is going to be even busier, flying back and getting all the necessary papers drawn up."

"I quite agree. It is late." The financier stood.

Tom was already standing, which left only Deborah seated. Belatedly, she rose, too. A hand settled on the curve of her waist, faint possession in its firmness. The burning contact of its warmth told her in advance that it belonged to Zane. Ostensibly his touch was innocent enough—to guide her from the lounge, but it sent a little pulse hammering in her throat. She was much too physically aware of him, all because of that one incident, and Deborah knew it had to stop.

"Good night, my polka partner." Foster Darrow clasped her hand in his stout fingers. "Be sure to have Zane bring you along the next time we meet."

"Of course," she murmured. "Good night."

The financier walked with them to the elevators in the hotel lobby. After a promise to be in touch within the next couple of days, he left and the copper-plated elevator doors swished closed to carry them to their suite of rooms. In total silence they made the ride to their floor. Deborah was bewildered by the lack of even mild jubilation.

Zane unlocked the door to their suite. It rivaled a spacious apartment in size. Besides three private bedrooms, there was a living room and dining room combined and a kitchenette tucked in a small alcove. Deborah remembered one of the first business trips she had taken with Zane, and her initial discovery that she was supposed to sleep in a bedroom in the same suite of rooms as Zane and Tom. At the time, she had wondered if she should request a private room on a different floor. All it had taken was one marathon session of paperwork that had lasted nearly all night, for her to appreciate the advantages of staggering from one room into the next to fall into bed. Besides, neither Tom nor Zane was given to nocturnal wanderings.

The hotel room door opened into the living room with its plush furnishings and even plusher carpet. Zane walked in and slipped the hotel key in his pants pocket. Deborah followed him, with Tom bringing up the rear. No one said a word.

"All this silence," Deborah finally burst out in disbelief. "Darrow said yes. Shouldn't we be celebrating or something? The way you two look, anyone would think he said no."

Zane didn't even acknowledge her comment with a glance, but Tom pivoted to look at her blankly for an instant. Then a wide grin split his face.

"Shall we polka?"

It was such a ludicrous suggestion that Deborah could only stare at him in amazed confusion. Before she could protest, Tom was swinging her into his arms and swirling her around the room in an absurdly exaggerated imitation of Foster Darrow, minus the benefit of music. The wild sense of humor of this apparently mild-mannered man had Deborah reeling with laughter.

"Stop, please," she begged, laughing so hard that she could barely breathe. When he had twirled her to the front of the apricot-colored sofa, he stopped to let her collapse on the cushions. "You're insane, Tom," Deborah declared as she wiped the tears from her eyes.

"Didn't you enjoy the dance?" He assumed an expression of mock regret, but the mischievous twinkle in his brown eyes belied it.

"You probably sounded like a herd of elephants stampeding, to whoever has the room below us," Zane remarked dryly.

"How can you say that?" Tom chided. "My partner is as light on her feet as a ton of concrete."

"Thanks a lot," she protested and lifted the mane

of copper hair away from her neck, letting the coolness of the air conditioner reach her damp skin.

"We *are* a little too matter-of-fact about Darrow's agreement," Tom said, sobering unexpectedly. "I guess Zane and I were thinking about all the work that was ahead of us, and all the different phases that have to be put in motion now that we definitely have a commitment on the financing."

"You are right," Zane agreed. "So is Deborah. We should be celebrating. Since it's too late for room service, why don't you go down to the kitchen, Tom, and bring up some sandwiches or snacks and a bottle of Dom Perignon?"

"Excellent suggestion," Tom asserted with alacrity.

"Here." Zane handed him some bills. "You might have to do some persuading."

"Right." He started for the door. "I won't be long. Keep the party going until I get back!" With a cheery wave, he walked out of the hotel suite.

His departure exposed an undercurrent of electricity in the atmosphere that Deborah hadn't been aware of before. Now she felt it tingling along her nerve ends. The few seconds of silence that followed ticked loudly in her head. Her gaze swerved from the door to meet the unfathomable blue depths of Zane's eyes. He held her look for an instant, then turned to walk casually to an oak credenza along one wall of the living room.

"For once your outspokenness was well placed, Miss Holland," Zane commented. "If you hadn't said something about celebrating, do you know what we would be doing now?" He slid her a lazy, sidelong glance, accompanied by a half smile that turned all her insides topsy-turvy.

"No." She shook her head, feeling the stiffness of her composure.

"We would probably be sitting at that table—" he nodded in the direction of the polished oak table in the formal dining end of the room "—and mapping out the completion schedule for different phases of the project, discussing permits and a half a hundred other details. Instead we are all going to relax for an hour or so, get some rest, and be fresh to tackle everything in the morning on the flight home."

"I hadn't thought about it like that."

"No, you followed your instinct. It was the correct one."

Deborah heard something click before Zane turned away from the credenza. He had taken several steps toward her before she heard the music and realized he had turned on the radio. By then he was standing in front of the sofa.

"Since Tom instructed us to keep the party going until he returned, will you dance with me if I promise not to ask you to polka?" He seemed to joke to take the seriousness out of his invitation.

What would he do if she said it was too dangerous to be in his arms, she wondered frantically. But how could she refuse when she had been the one to suggest they celebrate in the first place? No, Deborah knew she had to brazen her way through this moment as if she didn't care.

She forced out a laugh, "As long as that part about the polka is a promise, I'll accept."

Straightening from the sofa, she let herself glide

smoothly into his arms, pretending a nonchalance she didn't feel. This time Zane' didn't hold her at arm's length, but neither did he hold her close. Still, Deborah felt the disturbance of his nearness. It became essential to talk and not let the romantic music weave a dangerous spell around her.

"Tom continually amazes me," she declared. "On the surface he seems so quiet, but he's really a lot of fun, too. I'm probably not telling you anything you haven't already discovered. You've known Tom a long time, haven't you?" He seemed a safe subject.

"Yes." He ran his gaze over her brightly upturned face. "Are you and Tom having an affair?"

Deborah's first reaction was a startled, "What?" She followed it with an emphatic "No!"

"Is it so impossible?" His mouth quirked in a cynical line. "You are both unattached. You work together almost constantly. It would be natural for an attraction to spring up between you. Tom has a great deal of admiration for you. I have the impression the feeling is mutual."

"I do admire him," she admitted stiffly.

"But you aren't attracted to him?"

Her gaze was focused on the air beyond his shoulder. At the questioning sentence, her stormy gray eyes flashed an angry look at his face.

"If I was, would you suggest to him that he should go to bed with me to satisfy my libido?" she accused.

Deborah couldn't ignore the nasty suspicion that Zane was trying to steer her to Tom to avoid her becoming romantically attracted to him. It was totally unfair since he was the one who had made the advance the previous time. She had never encouraged

Zane to believe she found him sexually attractive. It angered her to think that Zane might believe she was yearning after him.

The humiliating thought made her attempt to twist angrily out of his arms. "That isn't what I meant at all!" Impatience surged through his clipped response as he immediately tightened his hold to keep her from escaping.

The pressure he applied jerked her back into his arms, its force carrying her into his chest. The contact caught both of them off guard. Their dance steps ceased as Deborah's head was tipped back to let her startled gaze drown in his possessive look. She was arched against his hard flesh and bone, stunned by his raw masculinity, and unnerved by the tremors quaking within.

"Zane." His name came from her lips in a voice that was half fearful and half wanting.

A muffled groan shuddered free of his throat as he lowered his head to savor the softness of her lips with his mouth. It was a slow, exploring process that melted her hesitancy. He adeptly coaxed her lips apart and probed the white barrier of her teeth until they, too, let down their defenses.

Her hand left his shoulder to curve into the virile thickness of his midnight-black hair and force his head down so she could know the full possession of his kiss. She was crushed to him, male hands igniting flames of excitement on the soft curves they caressed. She felt his mouth moving over her face, demanding and relentless, tantalizing and seductive by turns. Deborah pressed her hips more firmly against his thrusting thighs—needing, wanting, aching with the same primitive passions that burned him.

Incapable of coherent thought, Deborah could not reason out the right or wrong of her actions. She was dominated by the pure sensual impact of the embrace. The potent, masculine smell of him enveloped her senses. His mouth, hands, and tongue made her limbs weak with desire. The seething chaos of her emotions permitted only the urgent need to be part of this vital man to register on her mind.

Swept into the dangerous whirlpool of mindless passion, neither one heard the door being unlocked or opened. Tom's voice was cold water on the flaming embrace. "Refreshments are served on—" His bright announcement was abruptly broken off at the sight of them locked together, even as his words ripped them apart.

Deborah's face flamed scarlet under his shocked look. For a moment, nobody spoke or moved. Then Zane took a step forward, inserting himself between Deborah and Tom.

"I hope you brought some champange, Tom," he said in a remarkable even voice. "I think we all need a drink."

"Yes." Tom's voice was a thin thread at first, but gradually gained strength as he wheeled the serving cart into the room. "Yes, I have champagne. There is a tray of sandwiches here, too. Chicken salad, cheese, and ham. Potato chips and some sort of avocado dip."

Deborah almost wished Tom had asked all the questions she knew were buzzing in his head, but he was taking his lead from Zane and pretending he hadn't seen anything out of the ordinary. *God*, she thought wildly, *they don't really expect me to eat or drink anything, do they?* But Zane was already taking a cocktail sandwich from the tray and biting into it while Tom popped the cork on the champagne bottle.

"What will you have, Deborah?" Zane asked, shooting her a veiled glance to see if she had recovered.

At least he hadn't referred to her as Miss Holland. Deborah thought she would have broken into hysterical laughter if he had. She made her shaky legs carry her to the serving cart draped with a white linen tablecloth. She remembered some old saying about chalk and cheese.

"Cheese, I guess." Her hand trembled slightly as she took the little larger than bite-sized sandwich from the plate. It tasted like chalk when she bit into it. Then Tom was putting a champagne glass in her hand. She briefly met his eyes and saw the flash of concern in his gaze before he looked away.

"Here's to the new project." Tom lifted his glass in a toast.

They all clinked their glasses together and Deborah tried hard not to let her gaze linger on the strong, male hand with the sprinkling of black arm hairs curling out from beneath his shirt cuff. It was harder, still, not to remember that same hand had been caressing and molding her hips to his, only moments ago. The devastating force of his touch was still too vividly with her.

The next twenty minutes became a total mockery, a farce. Everyone talked about the project and the successful financing arrangements, but no one said a word about what was really on their minds. What remained unspoken filled the suite with a tension that scraped at Deborah's nerves.

Tom refilled his champagne glass and grimaced after taking a sip. "The champagne has gone flat."

"So has the party. We're all tired so why don't we call it a night," Zane suggested.

"Yes," Deborah was quick to agree. "We have to be up early in the morning so we can pack and fly home." She set her glass down, catching out of the corner of her eye the darting look Tom divided between them. She didn't give his suspicions a chance to form as she turned and tossed a careless good-night over her shoulder and walked directly to her private bedroom.

After closing the door, Deborah didn't bother to turn on the light. Instead she undressed in the darkness and slipped into her cotton nightgown. Tom's self-consciousness had been so obvious. She knew he had been wondering if she was going to sleep with Zane. She had no one to blame but herself for the direction his thoughts had taken. Deborah was well aware that she had been a very willing participant in that embrace that Tom had walked in on. If he hadn't returned when he did, she had the uncomfortable feeling that she might have been even more embarrassed.

Where was her control? She had always been a fairly level-headed person, never getting carried away by her emotions. Those terms certainly couldn't describe her behavior tonight. She was a bloody fool.

Zane Wilding was not only her employer but he was also a married man. What had possessed her?

As she climbed into bed, she heard the doors to the other bedrooms open and close. She stared at the ceiling. It wasn't going to be easy to sleep tonight, not the way her conscience was troubling her, and not with the realization that Zane was in the next bedroom.

Her arms felt so empty. Turning onto her side, Deborah pulled the spare pillow to her and wrapped her arms around that. It was too soft, its feel not at all reminiscent of the hard, male torso she ached to hold. She closed her eyes tightly and a hot tear squeezed out through her lashes.

CHAPTER SEVEN

ROOM SERVICE ARRIVED with three orders of a continental breakfast fifteen minutes after the wake-up call. Deborah took her coffee, juice and roll into her bedroom to have while she finished her packing. Zane and Tom would have theirs at the table, but she wasn't ready to face them. Besides, she had noticed the faint shadows under her eyes when she'd put on her makeup. It was an obvious betrayal of the sleepless night she'd spent. Secretly, she hoped the coffee and orange juice would have a reviving effect and chase away those shadows before anyone noticed them.

She drank her orange juice while she packed her cosmetics in their individual bag. The coffee was still too hot so she ate half of the Danish roll and threw the rest in the wastebasket. She was folding her clothes and placing them in the suitcase with meticulous care in order to prolong the whole process of packing, when there was a knock at her door.

"Who is it?" she paused, feeling something flutter in her stomach.

"It's Tom. May I come in?"

Deborah hesitated only a second before responding with an offhand, "Of course." She heard the click of the latch, but she didn't turn around.

"I called downstairs for a bellboy," Tom said, walking into her room.

"You can have my suitcases in a minute. I'm almost finished." She continued with her packing, smoothing the material of a skirt she had just laid into her suitcase.

"Deborah."

Something in his tone made her mentally brace herself. The muscles in her stomach knotted with tension as she held her breath. A splintering pain shot through her chest. She wished fervently that Tom would leave.

"Yes?" Deborah tried so desperately to appear absently curious as she gave him a brief glance over her shoulder before resuming the folding of her clothes.

He cleared his throat a little nervously. "I don't normally butt my nose into anybody's private life," he began.

"Then don't start now," she retorted, much sharper than she intended.

"This time it's different. It involves two people I care about a lot."

"Tom, don't." Deborah stopped pretending to fold the slip in her hands and clenched it tightly against her middle.

"I know this sounds like a line out of some old movie, but if I ever had a kid sister, I think she would have been like you. And I wouldn't be much of a big brother if I didn't warn her when I can see she's heading for trouble."

Her eyes were so dry they hurt. "Tom, honestly, I know you mean well and I'm flattered that you care about me, but I don't need a big brother. I—"

"Don't fall in love with Zane."

The blunt warning pivoted Deborah around. "I haven't." *Not yet anyway*, she qualified the thought.

"He'll never leave Sylvia. Not for you. Not for anybody." The sadness and firm conviction in his brown eyes reached out to her.

Deborah felt cold, icy cold inside and hopelessly empty. "I think I guessed that." Her voice wavered into a whisper.

"Don't get involved with him," Tom warned again. "His marriage to Sylvia will only tear both of you to pieces. You'll both be worse off than before."

"Yes," she swallowed the lump choking her throat. "I think I guessed that, too."

From the vicinity of the living room, there was the sound of someone knocking on the door to the hotel corridor. Zane called from another room. "Tom, that's the bellboy. Let him in."

"Right!" Tom shouted back, but paused to look at Deborah. "Are you all right?"

"I'm fine," she insisted. "I'm a big girl. I've weathered storms like this before. I can do it again."

"Chin up," he instructed with a lopsided smile and walked out of her room to answer the door.

THE PRIVATE LEAR JET was streaking across the sky, too high to cast a shadow on the Grand Canyon it flew across. Thunderheads billowed in the Rockies to the north, but the sky surrounding the jet was clear and the eastern horizon ahead was sapphire blue. The air was smooth. The only turbulence in the atmosphere was inside the plane.

Tom was seated at a desk in the plush interior of

the private jet, running up figures on his electronic calculator. In a cushioned armchair, Deborah was writing out a series of memos to be typed and sent to the various department heads when they arrived at the corporate offices later on. Each reference to Mr. Wilding that appeared in the memo caused her pencil to hesitate on the paper. It was caused by the wincing of raw nerves.

"How are you coming with those memos?" Zane stood beside her chair.

Her head jerked toward him, but not all the way, avoiding contact with his gaze. Deborah tried her professional voice. "I have two left." It worked admirably. "Did you want to dictate those alternatives to solve the environmental questions now? I can finish these later."

She didn't immediately get a response as he turned the chair in front of her around so that it was angled toward hers instead of away. As he folded his length into it, she couldn't help noticing the absence of his suit jacket and tie. The white of his shirt was stretched across his chest, hinting at the rippling muscles that bunched beneath it. Her pulse skittered in an erratic tempo. Taking his action as an affirmative answer, Deborah flipped to an empty sheet on her steno pad to begin taking down his dictation.

"The efficient Miss Holland." The grimness of his voice sounded almost censuring. Her startled gaze lifted to meet the hard glitter of his eyes. "She not only has her hair pulled back all primly in its bun, but she also has the waspish crispness back in her voice."

"I wear my hair in this style to keep it out of the way when I'm working," she began.

"It looks better loose," Zane interrupted, a muscle working in his jaw.

Oh God, she didn't want to know that. Taking a breath, Deborah glanced quickly down to the steno pad on her lap. He had leaned forward in the chair, which brought his face much too close.

"As for my tone of voice, I'll speak however I please. And wear my hair however I please," she asserted and kept her gaze firmly downcast. "Did you wish to dictate those alternatives, Mr. Wilding?"

"Deborah." His low voice carried a ring of exasperation along with a silent plea. But she refused to respond to the tug on her heartstrings. She wasn't his puppet. Determinedly, she kept all emotion out of her expression, aware of his searching gaze. At last, Zane let out a long sigh. In the limited range of her vision, she saw him flex his hands on his knees, then lace them together.

"Tom gave you a brotherly lecture this morning, didn't he?" The expectant tone of his voice said he anticipated an affirmative answer. Perhaps Tom had already admitted as much to him.

Deborah didn't see any point in denying it. "Yes, he did." She kept her answer very matter-of-fact.

"Tom is an intelligent, perceptive man. His counsel is always based on the soundest of reasoning. I've rarely known him to be wrong. He never gives advice unless he knows what he's talking about."

Zane seemed to be hammering his point home and a numbness inched through her at the invisible blows. She managed a terse, "I believe that."

Keeping her gaze averted from his face, Deborah wished he would get to the point and quit torturing her with all this talk that she didn't know how to take. If he wanted to get a message across to her, why didn't he just come right out and say it?

As if reading her mind, Zane asked a husky question. "Are you going to take his advice?"

Stunned by his unexpectedly frank question, Deborah's gaze jerked to his face. The probing search of his narrowed blue eyes explored the tormented uncertainty of her gray eyes. Wordless, she couldn't force an answer from her strangled throat.

The sculpted bronze of his features became taut with the strain of control. "Stay away from me, Deborah... for both our sakes."

Before she could respond to that crushing order, he was swinging out of the chair and striding across the carpeted floor of the aircraft. Resentment flared through her. How dare he put the burden of that on her? She had never been the one to make the first move. She had never flirted with him or invited his advances. Why was it her responsibility to make sure it never happened again? She was not a sultry temptress trying to lead him astray. She was the victim, not the seducer.

Tom intercepted her glaring look and sent her a quizzical glance. Deborah quickly avoided it, pretending she hadn't seen it and flipped back the pages of her steno pad to the memos she had been writing. She tried to bring her concentration back to bear the task, but she wasn't very successful.

SKIMMING THE PREVIOUS PAGE of the report, Deborah checked to make sure she hadn't omitted any facts as she combined three department studies into one overall view. She flexed her shoulders and back tiredly and felt a prickling sensation along her spine. She guessed the cause, her sensitive radar signaling its awareness of Zane's gaze on her.

In a quick, sidelong glance, she took note of the figure behind the large oak desk. Zane was leaning back in his chair, making no pretense of working. A haunting grimness shadowed his craggy male features and the winter steel of his eyes. The emotional strain of pretending there were no turbulent undercurrents between them became more than Deborah could take.

"Will you quit watching me?" she flashed in disturbed annoyance, fixing her frowning gaze to the pencil notes on her desk.

"It's after five. You can finish drafting that report tomorrow. You may go home, Miss Holland."

There was that dreaded "Miss Holland" again—so cold and so formal. It cut to the bone. Once she had worked until well after dark, but since that flight from California, Deborah began having what seemed like banker's hours. No more late nights. No more working until well after everyone else in the building had gone home. Only twice had she stayed late, and both times Tom had been there to act as a chaperon.

Deborah wanted to argue against his order to leave, but she invariably lost such battles. Instead, she reached down to pick up the slim, feminine briefcase she had recently purchased.

"I'll finish this draft tonight at home." Snapping open the case, she arranged the papers and notes inside.

"It isn't necessary." Zane rolled out of his chair

with a leashed sort of fury, even though his voice was evenly controlled. He walked to the small closet and removed her coat. "I'm not sending you home to work. You should be going out on a date."

He held her coat to help her into it. Deborah hesitated, then slipped her arms into the sleeves. "Maybe I should, but I don't happen to have a boyfriend or a lover to take me out."

It was a stiff, almost curt response. As he slid the coat onto her shoulders, his hands paused to clasp her bones. It was an inadvertently possessive grip that altered quickly into a kneading caress that made all her defenses melt. Deborah closed her eyes to savor the feel of his touch. All her sexual and emotional frustrations surfaced with a powerful yearning to have the promised fulfillment of his embrace.

"I think we're kidding ourselves," she declared in an aching whisper. "I should hand in my resignation and get as far away from you as possible."

"No." It was a choked protest that he shut his teeth on.

At the ring of the telephone, Deborah wrenched out of his hold to answer it, grabbing the receiver as if it were a lifeline. "Hello. Mr. Wilding's office." She heard the strained pitch of her voice, but there wasn't anything she could do about it now.

"Deborah? Is that you?" her mother's voice responded.

"Mom." Her startled recognition was followed instantly by alarm. "Is something wrong?" Deborah had never known her mother to call her at work before, so her first thought was that there was some emergency.

"Yes. I haven't talked to you in ages." Behind the amused voice was a thinly veiled reproof. "Since you're always at the office working, I decided if I wanted to hear your voice, I'd have to call you there."

"Actually I was just leaving to go home to my apartment."

Her eyes strayed to Zane, but he had turned his back to her, although Deborah knew he was listening. Would she have been on her way home if her mother had called a few minutes later? Somehow Deborah thought it was a question that she would never know the answer to. That charged minute when his hands had held her was gone. The fuse had blown and the lights had gone out.

"Do you have any idea how long it's been since I heard from you?" her mother asked.

"Didn't you receive the check I sent you this month?"

"Oh, yes," her mother admitted dryly, "I received the envelope from you with the check in it, but there wasn't even a scrawled note in it saying, 'I'm fine.'"

"I'm sorry, mother, but I've been . . . very busy."

"Is something wrong, Deborah?" In the shrewd question there was concern.

"No, of course not," Deborah denied that quickly.

"I know there is, but you obviously feel you can't talk to me about it. You must be having man trouble. Well, I guess you are old enough to work out your own problems, especially personal ones, so don't worry. I won't pry."

"Thank you, mother." Deborah didn't make any more of an admission than that.

"The main reason I called was to let you know that your brother Art is getting leave over Thanksgiving."

"He has! That's wonderful!" And her pleasure was genuine.

"Unfortunately I can't get any time off over the holidays, but I don't have to work the weekend before Thanksgiving. I thought we could have our family dinner on Sunday. Sarah and Barney can come then. Art plans to spend the Thanksgiving weekend with his girl friend in Boston. Can you come?"

"I'm sure I can make it. It'll be so nice to see Art. What about Ronnie?" Deborah asked about her other brother, also in the air force.

"He couldn't get a furlough, but he has his fingers crossed for Christmas. I'd love to talk longer, Deborah, but since you are on your way home, I'm sure you don't want to stay around the office much longer in case your slave-driving boss finds you something else to do to keep you later."

"You are right." *Partly, anyway.* "I'll be there the Saturday before so I can help you with dinner."

"If you patch up your differences with your man friend, bring him along."

"Don't count on that, mom. See you."

"Take care."

As Deborah hung up the phone, she turned to find Zane watching her, a lighted cigarette between his fingers. He glanced at the smoke curling from the tip, his expression unreadable. "I take it one of your brothers is coming home. Or is Art an old boy-friend?"

"My brother. He has a furlough over Thanksgiving, so we're all getting together for a family dinner the Sunday before." She didn't know why she was telling him.

"The weekend after next."

"Yes." *So soon,* she thought.

"You can have the Friday before off."

"There's no need," Deborah started to protest.

"It will give you time to pack whatever clothes and belongings you'll need for a month." Her mouth opened at the statement but Zane didn't give her a chance to ask where she would be going for a month—or why. "Instead of reporting back to work here on Monday morning, you can go directly to my country estate. Here are the directions." He ripped off a sheet of paper from the scratch pad on his desk and crossed the room to hand it to her.

"Your country estate?" Deborah looked at the directions blankly. "But why there?"

"Since my marriage, I have made it a custom to spend the holidays there. I don't see any reason to alter that tradition at this late date. Everything in this office will be transferred and we'll carry on our business as usual from there. A room is being prepared for you in the guest wing, since it would be impractical for you to drive back and forth. It is as spacious as your apartment, to assure you of maximum privacy while you're there." He paused in his aloof explanation to cast a cool glance in her direction. "Naturally, your meals will be provided. Do you have any questions about the arrangements, Miss Holland?''

"Not if you don't.'' The two of them under one roof for a month would be flirting with danger. Deborah knew it. Zane had to, as well. But if he was prepared to take the risk, she wasn't going to appear weak by running.

"Very well.'' He turned away and walked back to his desk. He never gave her another glance as he said, "Good night, Miss Holland.''

Tight-lipped, she didn't return the salutation as she gathered up her briefcase and purse and walked out of the office. This air of strictly business was a farce. One of these days it was going to blow up in their faces. Deborah had the feeling the explosion wasn't very far away.

IT WAS TEN O'CLOCK that evening before she put aside the report she was compiling. It was a demanding task to organize the data from three sources into a comprehensive and highly detailed summary. When the typescript began to blur, Deborah knew she had worked too long. But it had kept her mind off more disturbing subjects—like her boss.

Tense from all that concentration, she filled the bathtub with hot water and scented bubbles. She had barely relaxed in the luxury of a leisurely bath when the telephone rang. Deborah listened to the summons of the first half dozen rings and tried to be the kind of person who could ignore the telephone. On the eighth ring, she gave up the attempt and sloshed out of the tub to dash hurriedly to the kitchen wall phone. She didn't even stop to grab a towel, thankful she had closed the drapes previously.

"Hello?" She picked up the phone and waited for a response. When none came, she swore angrily at the unknown person who had hung up. "Damn!" But as she started to slam the receiver back on its hook, Zane's voice came over the line.

"Hello?"

The anger went out of her with a rush. "Yes."

"I didn't get an answer so I started to hang up, thinking you were gone," he stated.

"I was taking a bath," Deborah explained, a little of her irritation returning. "The trail of bubbles dissolving on my carpet would prove that."

His sharp intake of breath came clearly over the line. "Dammit to hell, Deborah! Why did you have to say that?" Zane muttered.

"I wasn't trying to be provocative, *Mr.* Wilding." She gave him a taste of his own formality, paying him back for all the times he had squelched her familiarity. "Why did you call?"

"Did you work on that report this evening?" At her affirmative response to his question, Zane informed her that there were two points that he wanted highly detailed. He went over them briefly, and asked if she had any questions.

"No. I believe I've already covered the specific areas you mentioned," she said, matching his crisp tone. "But I will check to be certain. Is there anything else?"

His pause lasted no longer than a heartbeat. "No. Nothing."

"Then, good night, Mr. Wilding." It helped the

ego to be the one who dismissed him for a change. She heard his clipped response just before the receiver settled onto its hook.

The evaporating bathwater had raised goose bumps on her skin, the scented bubbles drying and dissolving on her body. Shivering, Deborah hurried back to the bathroom. The water was only lukewarm. She rinsed the film of dried bubbles from her skin and toweled herself dry. There was nothing left but to go to bed.

CHAPTER EIGHT

THE DIRECTIONS Zane had given her were easy to follow. It was midmorning when she saw the black iron and red brick fences that marked the roadside boundary of his Connecticut estate. On one side of the road were pastures and the plowed ground of tobacco fields. Beyond the grillwork barrier there was the rolling expanse of a lawn splattered with the bright autumn colors of fallen leaves.

Red brick pillars towered on either side of the entrance. The scrolled iron gates stood open, as if waiting for her. Deborah followed the road that led through the trees to end in a cul-de-sac in front of an old colonial manor house. The sprawling two-storied house was built of red brick with white window and door casings. The front entrance was an impressive portico with white columns.

There was a narrow driveway that branched off the cul-de-sac; it apparently went to the rear of the house. Deborah debated whether she should take it, and decided instead to park in front of the house for the time being. She had barely stepped out of the car when the large white front door, with its brass knocker, was opened. A dark-haired woman in her late thirties stepped out. Dressed casually in slacks and sweater, she walked to the head of the short flight of steps leading to the porticoed entrance to greet Deborah.

"Hello. You must be Deborah Holland." The woman's smile was quick and ready, but there was a no-nonsense quality about her that earned Deborah's immediate approval. "I'm Madelaine Hayes."

Madelaine. Deborah remembered Zane mentioning that name, and always in connection with his wife. She climbed the steps and accepted the hand outstretched to greet her. Looking into the darkly intelligent eyes, Deborah had the feeling she was going to like this woman.

"I *am* Deborah Holland." She confirmed her identity. "And I'm glad to finally meet you. Mr. Wilding has mentioned you many times."

"But you don't know exactly who I am?" Madelaine Hayes guessed shrewdly.

"No," Deborah admitted with equal candor.

"I suppose you could say I'm a general factotum around here. My main responsibility is to look after Mrs. Wilding. I'm a psychiatric nurse." Those sharp brown eyes closely studied Deborah for a reaction to that announcement. It was unlikely that she expected Deborah to be surprised by her purpose in the house. Therefore, she must have expected that she suddenly might be treated as a servant. When there was no such reaction, she continued with hardly a break. "I also dabble in the housekeeping end, just to keep everything running smoothly for Zane."

Briefly Deborah wished she could refer to her employer with such casual familiarity, but there wasn't anything casual about their relationship. She preferred to change the subject entirely rather than respond.

"Should I leave my car parked there or drive it around to the back?"

"Leave it there. Frank—my husband—can drive it around to the garage after he's carried your luggage in." Madelaine dismissed the need for Deborah to move the car with a shrug of her shoulders. Guessing that Deborah probably didn't know her husband's role, she explained, "Frank manages the farm for Zane. Come on. I'll take you inside and show you your room." She turned toward the door she had left standing open. "Did you have any trouble finding the place?"

"None at all. Mr. Wilding's directions were very precise."

"They usually are. Do people call you Deborah or Debbie?"

"Deborah. I was never tagged with a shortened version, even as a child." Deborah crossed the threshold into the formal entryway of the manor house.

She looked around her with interest. The marble floor was enhanced by the rich luster of the hardwood wainscoting. Instead of the clutter of antiques that Deborah had expected, the foyer and wide hallway were simply furnished. Nothing detracted from the natural beauty of the house.

"I didn't have a nickname either. But what would they have called me? Maddy?" Madelaine Hayes joked and shuddered expressively.

A hand-carved, solid walnut door opened onto the foyer. Deborah turned toward the sound just as Zane stepped out. A different Zane than she had seen at the office. Instead of the elegant suit and tie he usually wore, he had a heavily ribbed sweater of ivory wool and black pants that hugged his muscular thighs. So blatantly virile, this new Zane had an immediate and devastating impact on her senses. He stopped abruptly when he saw her. His expressionless mask slipped, permitting her to see the leap of fire in his blue eyes. Much too quickly the look was gone.

"I see you have arrived safely, Miss Holland," he observed with apparent disinterest in the fact.

"Yes." Her heart gave a sickening lurch as Zane figuratively slammed the doors of welcome in her face.

"I was just taking Deborah to see her room," Madelaine explained. "I hope you aren't planning to put her to work until after she's had a cup of coffee and a chance to relax after her drive. You and Tom can hold the fort for a little while longer."

Deborah envied the brunette's ease in asserting herself. True, she, too, did speak out on occasions. Meekness was certainly not one of her qualities, but she lacked Madelaine's casualness. But obviously Madelaine had known Zane longer than she had. Plus she was married, which meant she didn't have the inner conflict of emotional attraction.

"An hour will be soon enough for you to report, Miss Holland," Zane stated after consulting his watch.

"In an hour," Deborah agreed stiffly.

"I'll make certain she doesn't get lost trying to find her way back to the study," Madelaine promised. "Did you want something?"

"Yes. Have Jessie bring us some fresh coffee." He started to turn to reenter the room he had just left when his wife's voice stopped him.

"Why wasn't I informed that a guest had arrived?" She spoke from the hallway, drawing all eyes to her.

A puzzled frown knit Deborah's forehead as she watched the petite blonde walk toward her. Sylvia Wilding held herself so stiffly, so erectly, putting one foot precisely in front of the other as if walking a tightrope, all the while facing straight ahead.

It wasn't until she heard Zane mutter in an angry underbreath to Madelaine, "Where the hell did she get the whiskey this time?" that Deborah realized the woman was drunk and trying very hard not to let it show.

"I don't know," Madelaine whispered back to him with a faintly incredulous note. "She must have some hidden that I haven't found yet."

"Welcome." Sylvia carefully walked to Deborah, ignoring her husband and Madelaine. "I'm sorry I wasn't here to greet you when you arrived."

"That's quite all right, Mrs. Wilding," Deborah assured her.

At the sound of her voice, uncertainty flickered across Sylvia's expression. "I have the feeling I should know you." Her face was devoid of makeup, exposing a sickly yellowish cast to her skin. Her blue eyes, glazed with drink, darted to Zane. "I should know her, shouldn't I?"

"This is Miss Holland, my assistant," he introduced them again.

"Oh. You aren't a guest then." She seemed to give up her pretense of sobriety and swayed unsteadily.

Madelaine was instantly at her side to put a supporting arm around her waist. Her attitude now was strictly professional. "I'll help Sylvia back to her room. Will you show Deborah where she will be staying?" she asked Zane.

"Yes." A nerve twitched near his eye, but it was the only indication that he wasn't pleased by the request. Without looking at her, he ordered, "This way," and started down the hallway.

Deborah had difficulty keeping up with his long strides, but she refused to ask him to slow down. Doors stood open along the way. She had a glimpse of a formal living room and a Tiffany lamp above a polished dining-room table. Zane made a right-angled turn to guide her into a different wing of the rambling house.

"You have a beautiful home," Deborah remarked, liking the little of it his hurried pace had permitted her to see.

"Fourteen years ago it was a home. Now it is just a house." His voice was hard and cold, rejecting her compliment. He stopped and pushed open a door. "This will be your room while you are here, Miss Holland." He stepped aside to let her walk in, but didn't follow her inside.

When Deborah realized that, she stopped and half turned. "Thank you for taking the time to—"

Rudely he cut her off. "If you want some coffee, the kitchen is the second door after the right turn. I'll expect you in the study in one hour."

"Yessir!" Her temper flashed at his flint-hard attitude.

He seared her with a narrowed look and pivoted

away from the door. After he'd gone, Deborah stood in the center of the room looking at the empty doorway.

"Damn you!" she breathed in the curse. It was hardly a whisper.

Turning from the door, Deborah forced herself to look at the room. It was spacious, with a color theme of pale lavender and blue. Besides a double bed and dresser, there was a sofa, armchair and a small desk. Near the window stood a small, circular table with two chairs. Of the two doors in the room, one led to a large bathroom, and the second was a walk-in closet.

"Hello." A man's voice called attention to his presence in the doorway. A tall, spare man smiled as he nodded to the suitcases he carried in his hands— her suitcases. "I would have knocked, but—"

"Come in. Let me help you." Deborah hurried forward to take one of the smaller cases he was juggling. "You must be Frank."

"That's right." He walked into the room and set her luggage on the floor. "I see Zane abandoned you to explore on your own."

"Yes." Her assessing gray eyes ran over the thatch of brown hair on his head, and the friendly, open expression of his thin face. She changed the subject. "This is a lovely room."

"The best we have. Zane insisted on that." His hazel eyes flickered curiously at her sudden tensing at the mention of Zane's name.

"That was thoughtful of him." Deborah was stiff. She knew it, but she couldn't seem to make herself indifferent to the subject.

Frank Hayes tipped his head to the side in a studying manner. "We knew Zane had a new assistant, but he never mentioned you were...so attractive. To be perfectly honest, we were expecting someone with thick glasses and about forty more pounds," he grinned.

"Intelligent is ugly." She tried to respond to his humor.

"Something like that, I suppose. Did Zane give you a rundown on the layout of the house?" he asked, turning his attention to more serious matters.

"He told me where the kitchen was so I could get some coffee."

"The house is U-shaped and the hallway runs the full length of it upstairs and downstairs," Frank explained. "All the rooms open onto the hall. You'll get confused by the number of doors, but just keep opening them until you find the right room. All the bedrooms are on the wing sides. There are only two rooms on this side that are occupied. Yours and Jessie's. Jessie is our cook and takes care of the house, along with some day help. Madelaine and I have our bedroom in the other wing where she can be close to Sylvia. Naturally, Zane's room is on that side. So is Tom's."

"I see," she murmured.

"There's a courtyard inside the U, and a heated swimming pool beyond it that we keep open all year."

"But what about when it snows?" Deborah gazed at him incredulously.

"As I said, it's heated. It's quite a sensation to go swimming when there is snow piled on the ground," he admitted.

"It must be," she agreed with fascination.

"Be sure to try it while you're here." Frank started toward the door. "I'll be putting your car in the garage behind the house. You can't miss it. It's the only building behind the house."

"Thanks for bringing my luggage in."

He shrugged away her thanks. "See you at lunch."

DEBORAH ADJUSTED QUICKLY to her changed environment. Everything from the office—every file, report and memo—had been transferred to the large study. Before the first day was over, she had everything organized and at her fingertips. The study was large enough to hold desks for her, Zane and Tom with room left over. Tom's presence helped to soothe the atmosphere, and the heavy work load helped assure that her attention wouldn't often get a chance to wander in other, disturbing directions. Everyone in the house, with the occasional exception of Sylvia Wilding, ate together, which offered a further buffer between Deborah and Zane.

By the time Thanksgiving morning dawned, Deborah had settled in so comfortably that it seemed as if she had been at Zane's country house longer than three days. Although it was a legal holiday, Deborah worked in the morning—as did Zane and Tom.

The midday meal wasn't served until one o'clock. The formal dining-room table was set with the best crystal, china and flatware. The centerpiece was a fruit-filled cornucopia. It was a lavish feast complete with stuffed turkey, sweet potatoes, two kinds of vegetables, three salads, and homemade rolls.

"Two Thanksgiving dinners in one year. You are

lucky, Deborah,'' Frank remarked as he took her plate and passed it to Zane who was carving the turkey.

"Yes, I am."

"What is your family doing today?" Tom asked, helping himself to a cranberry-orange salad.

"My mother is working. My brother is visiting his girl friend in Boston, and my sister is at her husband's parents'."

"I'm glad you are with us," Madelaine inserted. "Nobody should have to spend the holidays alone."

"Would you care for white or dark meat, Deborah?" Zane asked the question. While in the company of others, he adopted their habit of using her given name, but his cool tone kept her at a distance just the same.

"White, please."

"Ethan always wanted the drumstick. Remember, Zane?" The thin melodic voice of Sylvia Wilding, who hadn't spoken since she sat down at the table, swept an instant silence into the room.

The carving blade hovered above the browned breast of the turkey. A muscle tightened in Zane's jaw as he resumed the carving. "Yes, I remember."

"Most little boys do like the drumstick best," she continued with a dreamlike expression in her haunted eyes. "Ethan never could eat it all, of course, but we always gave him one. Did I tell you I saw Anna Blackstone the other day, Zane? Her little girl, Susan, was the same age as Ethan. She's eighteen now. Such a pretty thing. You wouldn't recognize her."

"No, I probably wouldn't," he agreed without

looking to the opposite end of the long table at the dissipated woman who was his wife.

"Have some sweet potatoes, Sylvia." Madelaine attempted to divert the conversation.

Sylvia didn't even see the casserole dish that was offered to her. Deborah's heart twisted at the forlorn look that passed over the drawn features.

"Ethan would be eighteen if he was alive." Tortured blue eyes focused their pain on Frank Hayes, seated on Sylvia's left. "I miss him. I miss my baby." Her voice broke on the last word. As if in pain, she clasped her arms across her stomach and began to rock gently back and forth in her chair. "I miss my baby so," she whispered over and over, her voice growing softer each time until finally only her lips were moving.

Madelaine pushed her chair from the table. The grimly resigned look she cast at Zane indicated to Deborah that the incident was not unusual. Probably more the rule than the exception. The brunette excused herself from the table and walked to Sylvia's chair.

"Come with me, Sylvia." Madelaine took hold of the rocking shoulders and helped the small blonde to her feet.

"I'll help you," Zane offered grimly, laying the carving knife and fork down.

But Madelaine shook her head in refusal. "It's better if you don't come, Zane."

His jaw tightened, but he didn't argue. Deborah gained the impression that Zane's presence somehow upset his wife. She remembered Sylvia's strident command that summer night long ago, for Zane not to touch her.

In a low voice Frank told his wife, "If you need me, just call out." Madelaine nodded a mute acknowledgment as she guided Sylvia out of the dining room. Sylvia's lips continued their silent movement. She appeared to be in some trancelike state.

Everyone's appetite seemed to vanish with Sylvia's departure. They went through the motions of eating, but no one did justice to the excellent fare before them, the incident casting a pallor on the feast of Thanksgiving. Afterward, Zane apologized to Jessie, the gray-haired cook.

"Aayah, it couldn't be helped," she agreed in her hard New England drawl. "But it's just that many more meals you're going to be having of turkey stew and casserole and turkey sandwiches."

No one complained at the prospect.

On Sunday of that Thanksgiving weekend, Deborah wandered into the informal morning room where everyone usually breakfasted. Only Madelaine was at the white table, sipping a cup of coffee.

"Good morning," she greeted Deborah with a quick smile.

"Good morning. Where is everyone?" Deborah sat in one of the white matching chairs, facing the window that looked onto the courtyard.

"Frank went to church. Zane is swimming, Tom must still be in bed. Coffee?" She held the spout of an insulated coffeepot above an empty cup.

"Yes. How is Mrs. Wilding this morning?" She hadn't seen Sylvia since Thanksgiving Day.

"She's talking again, but her depression is so deep," Madelaine sighed. "It's pitiful."

"Yes," Deborah fully agreed, then mused, "It's unfortunate they didn't have more children. Maybe she would have gotten over Ethan's death if they had." In a way it hurt to say that, but it was the thought on her mind so she said it.

"After Ethan was born, Sylvia couldn't have any more children. Frank was working for Zane then. He's told me how obsessive Sylvia was when it came to her son. She didn't want to let him out of her sight even as a baby. Zane had to force her to go out in the evenings without Ethan. It's a tragic irony that Sylvia was the one who was supposed to be watching Ethan when he drowned."

"Does she blame herself for what happened?"

"Yes, I suppose so." Madelaine shook her head, staring into the black surface of her coffee. "She had made Ethan her reason for living. When he died, I think she stopped caring about anything else."

"Even Zane," Deborah murmured.

"Yes, even Zane. A year after Ethan died, Zane tried to convince her that they should adopt a child. By then she had already started hitting the bottle. There wasn't any agency that would let them adopt a child when the mother was an alcoholic and mentally unsound. But Sylvia refused to discuss it with him. To this day, she won't even look at or talk to another child. She won't even acknowledge that they are in the same room."

"I suppose she thinks she would be betraying her son's memory if she let herself love—or even like—

another child," Deborah suggested and sipped at her coffee.

"Possibly," Madelaine conceded. "She is an alcoholic, but her problems are much deeper than that. I really have to admire Zane for the way he has stood behind Sylvia, never hating her for what she has done to herself and him." Her brown gaze slid to Deborah. "He is committed to her. You do know that?"

Stiffening, Deborah knew exactly what that look and that remark meant. "I've been warned about that before—by Tom, then Zane, and now you. Who's next? Frank?" Her question was tainted by amused bitterness. Obviously she wasn't very good at concealing her attraction to Zane.

"I hope you aren't going to pay any attention to those warnings," Madelaine's response was unexpected. "Zane needs someone like you. He can't keep living in a vacuum without love or without loving anyone. And I...I don't think that look I see in your eyes every now and then is one-sided."

"Maybe not." Her smile was jerky and wry. "But, as everyone has pointed out, there is no future in it."

"No one who is aware of the circumstances would condemn you or Zane for having an affair," Madelaine insisted. "As a matter of fact, every one of Zane's friends would approve of any woman who could bring some happiness into his life. He deserves it, if anyone does."

"Yes. Although I've never pictured myself in the role of the 'other woman.'" Deborah wasn't able to meet the older woman's gaze, but it was a relief to be able to discuss her feelings indirectly.

"Deborah—" Madelaine clasped her hand and

squeezed it with comforting reassurance "—love is a blessing, not a sin. Knowing Zane, you wouldn't be the 'other woman.' You would be the only woman."

"I wish...." But Deborah couldn't find the words to express what she was feeling.

"I know." The brunette laughed to break the serious atmosphere. "You wish I would shut up so you could have some breakfast. There's bacon, eggs, and toast in the warming pans on the buffet. Help yourself." Pushing her chair away from the table, she stood up. "I'll even let you eat in peace without me chattering in your ear. I have to check on Sylvia. See you later."

Deborah sat for several minutes after Madelaine had left, digesting all that had been said before she bothered with breakfast.

CHAPTER NINE

"FRANK AND I are putting the Christmas tree up tonight. Would you like to help us decorate it, Deborah?" Madelaine passed her the platter of roast beef.

"I'd love to. It's been years since I've done that—not since I lived at home," she admitted.

"We want to get the house all decorated before the dinner party tomorrow night. It is the Christmas season, two weeks removed," the brunette reasoned. "You can help, too, Tom. We'll put you in charge of stringing the evergreen boughs and the holly."

"Not the mistletoe, though," Frank inserted and smiled at his wife. "That's strictly my department."

"Which reminds me, Zane," Madelaine glanced down the table at the man sitting at the head. "With all the activity going on tomorrow night, I don't think I should leave Sylvia alone. So I won't be able to act as your hostess for the party. Deborah can stand in for me."

Deborah stared at her for a frozen moment, stunned by the bomb that had fallen. Then her widened gray eyes darted a look at Zane. He regarded her silently, a faintly warm light in his clear blue eyes.

"Would you mind?" he asked quietly.

"I'll help out, if you like," she agreed.

"It's just an informal get-together of some of my friends," he explained, sensing her hesitancy.

"None of them is as formidable as businessmen you've come in contact with, Deborah," Tom added, then winked, "and I can promise that none of them will ask you to polka."

"I like your friends already." She cast a laughing, sidelong glance at Zane. Her pulse quickened at the way he was looking at her, running his gaze over her russet hair hanging loosely over her shoulders. When his look lingered on her smiling mouth, Deborah had to look away, and Frank provided the perfect excuse.

"Hey! It's snowing outside!"

Big, fat flakes drifted to the ground beyond the windowpanes. Most of the flakes melted, but a thin covering of white was beginning to form. An outside light laid a bright path to illuminate the snowflakes against the gray black backdrop of night.

"Our first snow. Maybe we'll have a white Christmas this year," Madelaine added hopefully. "Build a fire in the fireplace tonight, Frank."

An hour later, a fire was blazing and crackling over dry logs. Madelaine had put on an album of Christmas carols to fill the living room with music. A tall, heavily branched Scotch pine tree towered in its tree stand in front of the paned windows facing out to the cul-de-sac driveway. The tree lights were all strung and Frank was plugging them in to make sure they all worked. Little fairy lights blinked on and off in perfect unison. Madelaine stood back and clapped. Deborah had a garland of silver foil draped on her arms so she had to voice her approval.

"It's beautiful, Frank."

"Don't praise him too much or it will go to his head," Tom warned with a teasing grin.

"You get back to work arranging those boughs on the mantel," Madelaine ordered, waving him about his business. "We'll take care of the tree."

It took the three of them—Deborah, Madelaine and Frank—to wind the bright garland around the massive Christmas tree. Deborah's glance kept straying to the walnut doors. Zane was in the next room, working. Her enjoyment of the task would have been complete if he had been there helping them. There had been times in the past two weeks when Zane had betrayed so much with just a look. At times he even acted friendly toward her. But he had certainly done and said nothing to encourage all the foolish yearnings that had begun to dominate her.

"Here are the Christmas ornaments." Madelaine set two large boxes on a side table and opened them. "You two get started while I see how Sylvia is."

"I'll check on her for you, honey," Frank volunteered.

The brunette hesitated, then agreed, "All right."

As he left the room, Deborah and Madelaine began hanging the brightly colored and decorated Christmas balls on the boughs of the tree. One box was soon emptied, but the second one went more slowly as they tried to find and fill in the empty patches. Deborah was stretching to reach a high branch devoid of any ornament when she heard someone enter the room. Automatically she presumed it was Frank returning, since he had been gone quite awhile. She couldn't quite reach the branch. When she tried to make it that last quarter inch, she lost her balance. A steel band hooked itself around her waist to keep her from falling against the tree.

"You almost knocked the tree over." Zane's huskily amused voice came right beside her ear.

His arm had stayed around her waist. Deborah was certain her knees would have buckled if it hadn't been for his continuing support. Her cheeks were flushed with the excitement of his touch as she tried to look backward to his face. All she could see was the point of his chin.

"I need to be a few inches taller to reach the higher limbs," she offered in defense of her near accident.

"I'll hang that for you. Where do you want it?" His arm released her from his hold to take the Christmas ornament from her hand. She hadn't even been aware that she still had it.

"On that branch." Deborah pointed to the one. Zane reached it easily. With his height advantage, he could reach all of the places that neither she nor Madelaine had been able to reach. She took three more ornaments from the box. "Put this one on the branch just above the blue ball," she instructed.

There was a laughing glint in his dark blue eyes, but he didn't object. When it was hung, he held out his hand for the next one. She debated briefly with Madelaine whether the green one would look better near the red one or the orange.

"By the red one," Deborah decided finally, and conveyed the order to Zane.

"You like telling me what to do for a change, don't you?" he mocked.

"I could get used to it," she admitted saucily.

His gaze caught and held hers for a breathtaking

second, a charge message of awareness flashing between them. In the fireplace, a log burned through and collapsed in a shower of sparks. It broke the silent communication between them and Zane turned to the tree to hang the ornament.

"That's the last one," Madelaine announced. "Tinsel time. Come on, Tom. You can help."

He had finished arranging the nativity scene inside the garland of evergreen boughs and holly leaves woven along the edge of the fireplace mantel. He had been sitting in a wing chair watching their efforts. At Madelaine's prompting, he rose to join them. She divided the packets of long, silver foil among the four of them. They tossed it on the tree until it shimmered and gleamed in the multicolored blinking lights.

Stepping back, they all paused to admire the finished product. The mighty pine tree was bedecked in holiday finery, glittering and sparkling, just waiting for gifts to be spread beneath its limbs. Something brushed her hair and Deborah turned.

"You had tinsel in your hair." Zane held up the thin strip of foil to show her. With a glance she acknowledged its existence, before her gaze was compelled to return to his face.

Tom murmured something and Madelaine breathed a hurried, "Ssh." Deborah saw Zane's gaze flicker upward and followed it to the sprig of mistletoe dangling above them.

"It seems we are well and truly caught in the old holiday custom. . . ."

As his murmuring voice hesitated, Deborah warned him, "Don't you dare call me Miss Holland."

"Deborah," he finished, a light dancing in his eyes.

He lightly brushed his mouth over hers and Deborah felt him tremble. But Zane didn't increase the pressure of his kiss before he lifted his head. She wanted to cry out in frustration, but her expressive gray eyes said what her voice couldn't.

"Cocoa time." Frank returned to the room, carrying a large tray with five steaming mugs of hot chocolate balanced on its surface. "I stopped by the kitchen and persuaded Jessie to fix this for us. She even volunteered a plate of her Christmas cookies."

"You certainly timed it right," Madelaine declared and cleared the empty boxes off the side table so he could set the tray on it. "We just finished the tree."

"It looks great. I knew if I waited long enough you would have it all done," he grinned.

Taking a mug of cocoa and a cookie, Deborah curled up on the alpaca rug in front of the fireplace. Zane chose the chair that flanked the fireplace on her side, while Frank and Madelaine sat on the sofa that faced it. Tom remained standing, leaning a shoulder against the mantel and munching on a cookie.

"Does your family usually celebrate on Christmas or Christmas Eve?" Madelaine asked, directing her question at Deborah.

"On Christmas."

"I presume you are planning to go home for Christmas." Zane's curt statement held an undercurrent of challenge. Deborah reacted with prickles of defiance that she tried to disguise. She shifted her position on the rug to bring his chair into her view, tucking her feet beneath her to sit cross-legged.

"Yes, I am." Her gray eyes coolly met his shuttered look, the hard-grained lines of his face hinting at a grim displeasure. "My youngest brother, Ronnie, has a furlough to come home for the holidays. Since my mother had to work on Thanksgiving, she'll have Christmas day off. I know Christmas falls in the middle of the week this year, but it isn't a long drive from here to New Haven. I can leave on Christmas Eve and come back late Christmas day, which shouldn't interfere too greatly with your work schedule."

"I wasn't suggesting that you couldn't have the time off," he clipped out the response.

"Oh?" The taunting inflection of the one word doubted him.

"I was thinking of the heavy traffic."

"I'm a competent driver," Deborah insisted. His gaze slid to the small, red scar on her left arm. "That accident was not my fault!" she flared.

"Accidents rarely are the victim's fault, but they get hurt just the same," Zane countered in a stiffly controlled voice.

"I'm willing to take the risk."

There was an impatient thinning of his mouth. "You always are. I don't think you ever listen to anyone."

"I don't know about that," Deborah retaliated. "You told me to stay away from you and I have been." She saw the fiery blue glitter of his gaze arc from her to remind her they weren't alone in the room. Her temper wouldn't be silenced by their quiet, onlooking faces. "I'm not saying anything they haven't guessed. They've warned me about you, too."

Her bold anger had goaded Zane beyond endurance. Striking with the swiftness of a jungle animal, his fingers curled painfully into the soft flesh of her arm, and half pulled Deborah out of her sitting position.

"I'd like to shake some sense into your head," he threatened in a savage underbreath.

"Why don't you?" she challenged, her throat dry and aching. "I could definitely use some."

Her arm was released and in one fluid motion, Zane rose from the chair and took three strides to the table where he set his cocoa mug on the tray. Deborah stared at the broad set of his shoulders. His back was facing her, shutting her out again and denying the unspoken feelings that existed between them.

Madelaine was saying something, but Deborah couldn't hear the words above the deafening roar of her heartbeat. On the record player, a new selection began playing. Zane turned his head to look at her. Something in the haunted shadows of his blue eyes made her listen to the words.

I'll have a blue Christmas without you.
I'll be so blue thinking about you.
Decorations of red on a green Christmas tree
Won't mean a thing if you aren't here with me.

The sharp breath she took went no farther than the lump in her throat. As if he regretted letting her have that little glimpse, the shutters came down to block out his thoughts. Zane abruptly turned aside.

"I have some work to finish up," he announced to signal his departure. Pausing, he sliced a look to

Tom. "Where is that computer analysis of the year-end report for the Gillingham Company?"

"It's—never mind. I'll get it for you," Tom moved away from the fireplace to follow Zane out of the room.

The heat from the crackling fire warmed her back, but still Deborah shivered. Her gray eyes darted an uneasy look at the couple seated on the sofa. She uncrossed her feet to stand, staring down at the mug her nervous fingers clutched.

"I'm sorry if I embarrassed you," Deborah apologized. "I know I shouldn't have made such a scene, but—" What was her excuse? The turmoil of churning emotions made her restless and on edge.

"You don't have to apologize," Frank offered.

"I think you did the right thing," Madelaine added and ignored the shushing look her husband gave her. "No, I mean it. You were right to force it out in the open, Deborah. It's time Zane stopped hiding it."

"Thanks for trying to make me feel better." Deborah appreciated their efforts, but there was only one person who could ease her torment and he had walked out of the room. She moved to the window by the Christmas tree where a heavy swirl of snowflakes whipped at the glass panes.

"Well? Zane may work all night if he wants," Frank declared, slapping his wife's knee as he pushed himself upright from the sofa. "But I'm going to get some sleep."

"It's been a long day for me, too," Madelaine agreed, rising to join him. "I'll check on Sylvia first, though."

Neither sleep nor the emptiness of her bedroom sounded inviting to Deborah. She was much too agitated and tense. She had an excess of energy that needed to be burned off, not bottled up by inactivity.

"Good night, Deborah," Madelaine said, and Frank echoed her words.

Snow, activity, and Frank sparked an idea. Deborah pivoted from the window. "Frank, do you remember what you said about swimming when there was snow on the ground? Would it be all right if I used the pool tonight?"

He stopped short, staring at her as if she'd lost her mind. "Alone? I don't think that would be wise. The snow will be here tomorrow."

But Zane will have me slaving away at the desk tomorrow, Deborah thought, but she didn't argue against his advice. "I suppose you are right," she sighed in regret. "Good night." She walked over to pick up the tray of empty hot-chocolate mugs. "I'll take these to the kitchen and save Jessie a trip."

"Are you going to your room?" Frank asked.

"Yes." It didn't make any difference which empty room she prowled. She'd pace the floor in either so she might as well confine her restlessness to her own bedroom.

"We'd better unplug the tree lights then." He walked back to do it while Madelaine waited for him. Deborah left the room before they did.

No one was in the kitchen so Deborah washed up the cups rather than leave them for Jessie to do in the morning. Finally, she had no more reason to postpone going to her room.

The blankness of the television screen greeted her

when she entered. It offered a spectator form of entertainment to while away the time, but it wasn't what she wanted. The small desk reminded Deborah that she owed her sister a letter, but she'd been sitting at a desk all day. The marble tub in the bathroom offered to relax her. Deborah turned away from its invitation with a sigh of dissatisfaction. The wide expanse of the double bed yawned at her. The last thing she wanted to do was lie down.

A sharp knock at the door spun her around, catapulting her heart into her throat at the unexpected noise. Deborah swallowed it down and crossed the room to answer the summons. Zane stood in the hallway when she opened the door. Quicksilver tongues of fire raced through her veins.

"Frank mentioned you wanted to go swimming." Wasting no time on preliminary greetings, Zane went straight to the point with a curt explanation of why he was there. "I wasn't sure you would take his advice about not swimming alone."

"So you had to come and check," she issued tightly, a thin thread of sarcasm lacing her words. "As you can see, I'm here. Satisfied?"

"Yes," he snapped. "It's better than wondering if you've cracked your head and are floating face down in the pool."

"Such concern for my welfare," Deborah mocked him. "How touching."

Anger blazed in his eyes, but his clenched jaw kept it back. "You have fifteen minutes to change into your swimming suit and meet me at the rear entrance." Zane had barely issued the order before he walked away, leaving Deborah to gape after him.

When she recovered from her astonishment at his invitation, one minute had already gone by. She raced to change her clothes and make up for the lost time. Her culotte robe of French-blue knit offered a perfect covering for her swimsuit and protected her from the elements, as well. Deborah slipped her feet into a pair of flat shoes and hurried down the hallway to the rear entrance. Zane was already standing there, waiting for her.

"I'm ready," she said in a voice that was slightly breathless from her haste.

There wasn't a response as Zane turned the knob of the door that opened onto the courtyard. He switched on the flashlight he was carrying and a beam of light picked out the snow-covered path through the courtyard.

It was still and quiet outside, the falling snow making no sound as it coated the ground white. Since Zane had the flashlight he led the way and Deborah followed. It was pitch-black except for the light cast from the house windows.

"The pool was never intended to be used at night so there aren't any lights," Zane stated to explain the blackness ahead of them, except for the gauze curtain of white flakes. "There should be enough light reflected from the house to enable us to see."

It was a matter-of-fact statement. There was nothing in his tone or attitude that invited discussion. Deborah wasn't certain whether it was the coldness of the air penetrating her robe or his icy attitude that made her shiver. She noticed the sprinkling of snowflakes melting to crystal drops on his jet black hair. A cynical thought crossed her mind—that it was amazing the snow melted on a man made of ice.

The flashlight beam shone on a strip of concrete devoid of any snow cover, although it glistened wetly. Beyond it, a vaporous mist hovered on the surface of the pool, the heated water creating steam.

"Watch your step," Zane instructed. "The concrete deck around the pool is heated to keep ice from forming, but it will be slippery from the melted snow."

His words of caution were indifferent and he didn't offer her the steadying support of his hand. Walking carefully, Deborah followed him onto the wet cement deck. He stopped in front of a small shed that housed the pool's filtering system.

"We can leave our clothes in here so they'll stay dry." He opened the door and propped the flashlight against the side of the building, its beam dimly illuminating the pool area.

Snowflakes flitted around him as Zane stripped off his sweater. The cold had begun to numb her fingers so that they fumbled stiffly with the zipper of her culotte robe. At least, Deborah blamed it on the cold rather than on the disturbing sight of the rippling muscles of his shoulders and back. Without ceremony, Zane stepped out of the trousers that covered his black swim trunks. Bundling his clothes and shoes together, he set them inside the small shed.

His sideways glance barely touched her before he took a step toward the pool and knifed soundlessly into the water. The concrete was warm beneath her bare feet, but Deborah felt the nipping chill on her exposed flesh. Shivers danced over her skin as she hurriedly folded her robe around her shoes and set them in the shed beside his clothes.

She walked to the pool's edge and hesitated. She didn't want to dive into the water until she knew where Zane was. He surfaced in the middle of the pool, his wet hair gleaming like black satin in the swirling white vapor. Facing her, he treaded water. Under his hooded regard, Deborah became conscious of the brevity of her two-piece flowered suit.

"Quit posing before you freeze to death." His taunting voice prodded her.

"I wasn't posing," she denied. "I didn't know where you were and I didn't want to jump in on top of you."

"You know where I am now."

Her teeth had begun to chatter from the cold; otherwise Deborah would have made a suitably cutting retort. Instead, she fluidly dived off the side, making a graceful entrance into the water, even if it lacked his finesse. The heated water was a delicious shock to her chilled skin. Deborah surfaced not far from Zane, flinging her hair out of her face with a toss of her head and smoothing it backward with her hands.

"This is marvelous," she declared in amazed delight. "It's almost as warm as bathwater."

"You like it, do you?" A smile almost let itself be seen as his look became gentle.

Her full appreciation of the experience was just beginning. She turned in the water, looking around her. While she was enveloped in warmth, everything outside the pool was wearing winter's white coat. The foglike mist floating above the surface of the water added to the magical wonder, creating a dreamlike quality to make the moment unique unto itself. Deborah turned her face to the black sky to let the snowflakes drop wetly on her lashes, nose and mouth.

"It is fantastic!" She was repeating herself, but it didn't seem to matter. "No wonder you didn't bother to enclose the pool. This is sensational!"

The flashlight propped upward at the pool side gave just enough light so that Deborah could see the snow frosting the bare branches of the shrubs and trees. Everything was being transformed to white with winter's breath while she was swimming in water as warm as summer.

"A lot of ski resorts have heated pools or hot springs for their guests." Zane denied that his was unique.

"Yes, but they are for tourists and they would be crowded with people. This is private—with only the snow and the sky and the mist." Deborah spoke softly, as if talking about intimate companions.

Zane abruptly changed the subject. "Do you want to make a few laps of the pool?"

Part of her wanted to tread water and marvel at the scene, but the energy within her demanded to be released. "All right."

She struck out for the far end of the pool with a strong but leisurely crawl. Zane kept pace beside her, shortening his stroke that could have easily outraced her. They covered the length of the pool four times before Deborah clung to the side in exhaustion. Zane was two lengths into the fifth lap before he realized she had stopped.

"You aren't quitting already, are you? We've just started." The glint in his eyes mocked her.

She had deliberately stopped at the shallow end where her feet could touch the bottom, but her fingers curled into the cement lip of the pool to keep her balance. She was winded from the four previous laps and wasn't about to try a fifth.

"You may have just begun, but I'm finished," Deborah countered in a voice breathless from her exertion.

A low chuckle came from his throat, but he didn't say any more. For a brief second, he straightened in the water, giving Deborah a glimpse of his powerful, trim-lined physique—the broad shoulders and narrow hips of a swimmer. Then he pushed forward for the opposite end of the pool. He disappeared into the mist, but she could hear his strokes cleaving the water.

CHAPTER TEN

UNTIL HER BREATH RETURNED, Deborah drifted along the edge of the pool Zane continued his laps across the pool's length while she was content to enjoy her surroundings. Flat flakes continued to rain from the darkened sky and mix with the white steam rising from the heated water.

Staying close to the side of the pool, she began a slow backstroke. She was careful to avoid the center area where Zane was, not wishing to interfere with his swimming. The novelty of floating in warm water while all around her it snowed, had not worn off. An enchanted spell had been cast, it seemed.

"Keep your fingers together and make a cup of your hand. You'll have a stronger stroke."

Zane's voice came out of the mist, startling her. Deborah stopped swimming and tried to come upright, not realizing she had left the shallow end and ventured into deep water. As her legs stretched for the bottom, she went under with a sputter of surprise. Immediately, she kicked for the surface and came up coughing. An arm went around her and Deborah clutched at the water-slick flesh of a muscled shoulder. With a powerful kick, Zane propelled her toward the pool side while she wiped her face and coughed out the water she had swallowed.

"Are you all right?" His arm remained curved around her middle.

"Yes," she nodded quickly and gulped in air.

The smoothness of the concrete side was against her shoulder, but Deborah didn't remove the hand that circled his neck. Pushing the wet strands of copper hair out of her eyes, she flashed him a smile of chagrin.

"I didn't realize the water was over my head there," she admitted.

"Obviously," Zane murmured dryly.

While his arm continued to support her, his other hand gripped the edge of the pool to keep them at the side. Recovered from her accidental dunking, Deborah felt the first glimmer of silken awareness. Long, muscled thighs were floating against hers, masculine and firm in their contact. Her hip was drifting inside the cradle of his. The thin, wet material of her swim suit top didn't lessen the sensation of her breast rubbing against the hairy manliness of his chest.

Her eyes sought his face, sensual tension tightening her stomach. The brilliant blue of his gaze was watching the rapid pulse beating at the base of her throat. Slowly his eyes lifted to look into hers. They mirrored all the turbulent emotions that were quivering through Deborah.

The hand on her back tightened and it was all the invitation she needed to glide toward the strong, male outline of his mouth. When it parted to consume her lips whole, heat scorched through her limbs, making a mockery of the temperature of the water they floated in.

While her left hand continued its possessive encirclement of his neck, her right curled its fingers into the wet, silken texture of his black hair. Compulsively Deborah shaped her body to his hard torso. The contact seared her with a longing for fulfillment that couldn't be denied. She ached to be a part of him with a fire so intense it was out of control.

"We're in water over our heads." His mouth moved against her lips to speak the words, his voice husky and rasping, betraying his aroused state.

"I don't care if I drown." If this was what it was like, it would be sheer heaven, swamped by desire and awash with a bottomless love. A muscled leg sliced its way between hers to brace itself against the concrete side of the pool below the water. A violent tremor quaked through her body. Deborah felt the muscles in his shoulders ripple in a constricting movement. His mouth hardened on hers in a mute promise to return before it pulled away.

"Hang on," he ordered and used the leverage of his arm and leg to push away from the pool side.

Automatically, Deborah linked her fingers together behind his neck. The steel grip of his hand on her waist kept her almost on top of him as he pulled her along with him. The powerful stroke of one arm combined with the kick of his legs to carry both of them toward the shallow end of the pool. Their eyes were locked together.

Deborah knew she would trust herself in the stormiest seas with this man. In his arms, she could ride out the roughest gale. There was nothing so insurmountable that they could not face and conquer together. He was not some god who would offer her paradise. He was made of sinew and bone. Loving him would be alternately heaven and hell, but Deborah wanted a life sentence.

When Zane stopped in shallower water, it lapped at his shoulders, but her toes were barely able to scrape the bottom. Not that it mattered. Deborah preferred to hang onto him and have the strength of his body support her. It was impossible to get too close. Now both of his hands were free, no longer hampered by the necessity to keep them afloat. They pulled her buoyant weight firmly inside the circle of his arms and pressed her curves to his unyielding flesh.

His mouth was driving in its possession of her lips, parting them to let the sensual probe of his tongue fire her senses with its demanding claim. It raged through her with primitive force, sending quivers of joy deep into her soul. But Zane wasn't satisfied just to stake his ownership of her mouth. He began branding her face and throat with kisses. Deborah returned them with equal fervor, pressing her lips against his vital skin and tasting the chlorine-tainted flavor of him.

Behind her neck, she felt his fingers tug at the knot of her halter strap and untie the wet bow. His hands trailed halfway down the sensitive skin over her spine to unhook her top and free her breasts from their confinement. Deborah didn't even notice the top half of her swimsuit floating aimlessly away from them. Her senses were aflame with the sensation of the naked globes of her breasts crushed to his bare, muscled chest.

Then his hands were gripping her waist and lifting her weightless body partly out of the water, while his mouth made an initial foray down the damp valley between her breasts. Her fingers curled into the bulging muscles of his shoulders to steady herself, her nails digging into his flesh at the tantalizing ascent of his lips to a rosy peak. Crystalline flakes of snow melted on her enraptured face, bestowing her with nature's sweet kisses.

The steel bands of his arms slid around her, one circling her waist and the other curving under her bottom to mold the lower half of her body to the muscled tautness of his stomach. His licking tongue ignited a liquid fire that spread quickly through her veins, consuming her with a molten heat that melted her bones. Deborah shuddered with a wild need.

His hold loosened, letting her slide down to his level. The disturbed blue of his gaze scanned the love-drunk look in her gray eyes. Her lips trembled for his kiss, but Zane denied her its satisfaction to rest his forehead against hers, closing his eyes. Her consolation was the caressing warmth of his heavy breath against her skin.

She savored the moment, letting her hands glide over the powerful muscles of his shoulders, and wander down to let her fingers curl into his springy chest hairs. Zane had claimed his ownership of her body. Now Deborah was claiming her right to his. Her touch produced a shudder that quivered through him. The circle of his arms grew smaller as he molded her more tightly against him and pressed his mouth to her cheekbone.

"Do you know what you are doing to me?" Zane breathed the tortured question into her ear.

"I...hope the same thing you are doing to me."
Her whispered answer was equally revealing.

What little breath she had was taken from her as the
hand at the small of her back slid under the elastic
band of her swimsuit, pushing it down. The wet material clung stubbornly to her skin, requiring the assistance of a second hand. Deborah floated free of his
arms as the last barrier was banished to the pool. She
trod water several feet from where Zane stood. The
darkness and the water hid her body from his eyes.
Deborah felt a shameless twinge of regret. A wanton
part of her wanted Zane to look on her and be pleased
by her womanhood. They drifted closer, lessening the
distance that separated them without eliminating it.

It was not an attempt to prolong the agony of
wanting each other. Rather, it was a savoring of all
that had led up to the moment to come when intimate
discoveries would be made. There was no need to
rush. The anticipation was sweet and heady, an
aphrodisiac to the senses.

"I've wanted you for a long time, Deborah." He
moved closer, the strong, male lines of his face clearly visible in the dim light. Vital and compelling, his
sun-bronzed features sent her heart racing. "Not just
because you are a beautiful, exciting woman, although you are that." His voice was a husky caress as
warm as the water that sensually engulfed her naked
form. "I've been tempted to make love to a lot of
women out of sheer sexual necessity. I craved the
satisfaction their bodies permitted, but not them. I
thought it would always be that way."

"Isn't it?" She wasn't trying to be provocative;
her voice was as huskily disturbed as his.

"You know it isn't," Zane insisted in a mocking growl. "You got under my skin. You with your rusty brown hair—" his hand came out of the water to tug a long, wet strand "—and your eloquently expressive gray eyes that so often burned me with their silver flames. When you first came to work for me, I tried to freeze out your anger, but you continually riled me with your sharp tongue and censuring looks. I tried, but I couldn't be indifferent to you. I should have realized it was a warning."

"I didn't recognize the danger signals either." Her finger traced the crevice in his cheek near the corner of his mouth. "Considering the way the sparks flew when you rubbed me the wrong way, I should have known what would happen when you rubbed me the right way."

His hand slid to clasp her forearm. He kissed the inside of her elbow, then the small scar. "It wasn't until your accident that I fully realized what you had come to mean to me. The hospital said you weren't badly hurt, but I had to see for myself. When I walked into that emergency room and you called me by my name, if the doctor hadn't been there I would have made love to you on the spot."

"I called you Zane?" she said in surprise. "I don't remember that. Is that why you finally called me Deborah?"

"I'd been thinking of you as Deborah for weeks before that." His hand glided up her arm to caress her neck and the hollow of her throat.

"All I remember is how cruelly you pointed out that my services were not indispensable," Deborah murmured, her breath catching as a finger teased the sensitive area near her ear.

"Your services were not indispensable, but you were. It shook the hell out of me to admit that. I had to send Tom over to see if you were okay that night because I didn't trust myself alone with you." Zane's mouth seemed to grow jealous of the privileges his hands were enjoying and moved to take its place to continue the stimulating exploration of her neck and earlobe. Their bodies drifted against each other in the water. "The night you taunted me for not responding to Sylvia's needs provoked me into showing how much I needed you. I came very close to insisting that you provide my satisfaction as part of your job—anything to have you."

"I didn't want you to stop that night," Deborah admitted, closing her eyes as his warm lips moved over her lashes. "The only reason I said that was because I was afraid of being the other woman in your life."

"The other woman." There was amusement in the breath he exhaled. "You are the only real woman in my life. The only one." Zane briefly teased her lips, his white teeth tugging at the lower one for an instant. "When you and Tom were doing that ridiculous dance in the suite, I was overwhelmed with jealousy. The idea that you and he might be having an affair nearly drove me out of my mind. Just to see you laughing with him—"

She heard the taut pain in his voice and quickly stopped him. "Tom is a great guy—wonderful and kind and gentle. But I was never attracted to him. Next to you, he...." Deborah laughed softly. "I'm not saying any more or I'll add to your conceit."

"My conceit!" He bruised her lips with a punishing kiss that soon hardened with passion.

With a faint moan, she wrapped her arms around him, wanting to become absorbed by his vital, male body. She gloried in the strength that pulsated through his rock-firm flesh and the hair that was rough against her breasts. She was excited by the taste of his tongue, the feel of his hard muscle, and the smell of his virile scent. It quivered through her every fiber with endless longing.

Steam swirled around them, generated from the combination of their body heat and the warm water of the pool. Snow melted into crystal droplets on their skin and hair, but they were too engrossed in each other to notice the tiny snow beads. Lips were busy kissing, teasing, and demanding while hands caressed, explored and aroused willing flesh. Love was a hot flame that burned them together.

"Zane," Deborah whispered his name, loving him so intensely it was a pleasurable ache. Tears of boundless happiness were on her cheeks mingling with the snow drops. "Why did you bother to tell me to stay away from you? Didn't you realize that it was already too late? Why did you put us through all this frustration; waste all this time?"

"I'm married." He dragged out the words as if they were torture. There was a fierceness in the way his hands cupped her face as if he were afraid of losing her.

"Tell me something I don't know," she smiled because it didn't make any difference. It seemed more of a sacrilege to pretend that it did.

"You don't understand," Zane insisted in a heavy

sigh. "There are so many things I can't give you."

"I only want you. I'll be satisfied with that." Her voice trembled with strong undercurrents of emotion.

"Will you? I don't know that I'll be satisfied." His searching gaze probed deeply into her eyes. "I know there will come a time when I'll want to see our child at your breast." He lifted her to bend his head and kiss the swelling curve of her breast, cupping the underside with one hand. Deborah quivered as he straightened. "Would you want to have my child?"

"No." She swallowed the happy lump in her throat. "But I'd love to have your children." She lightly stressed the change to the plural form.

She heard his sharp intake of breath before she was crushed hard inside his arms in an embrace that was brutal joy and aching regret. Deep shudders wracked his shoulders and Deborah tried to absorb his inner pain.

"Yes, I would undoubtedly want children," Zane admitted in a quivering breath. "But I couldn't give them my name."

"You could give them your love. You would be their natural father. You could even legally adopt them," Deborah argued gently. "Don't put obstacles in our path to keep us apart. I'll just knock them down."

"I couldn't stand it if people looked down on you, Deborah," he muttered thickly.

"I couldn't stand it if you walked away from me— not after this. There has to be a way for us to be together." There was a desperate catch in her voice, a tiny thread of alarm.

"We'll find one...because I can't let you go."

"You couldn't if you tried, because I wouldn't let you."

His mouth twisted wryly as he lifted his head. "I can't think straight when you are in my arms." He loosened his hold, but Deborah resisted.

"Don't think," she protested.

"No. I need to think this out." His hard jaw was set in a determined line.

"But—"

"Zane!" Tom's shout intruded on the moment. "There is a long-distance phone call for you from California. It's important."

Together they turned in the direction of his voice. A flashlight beam zigzagged across the pool's surface until it found them. Deborah blinked and turned sharply away from the harsh glare, lifting a hand to shield out the spot of light.

"I suggest you point that light in another direction, Tom," Zane warned. "This bold woman with me might not be embarrassed but I'll be jealous as hell of what you might see."

"Zane!" Deborah hissed.

At the twin flags of pink on her cheeks, Zane laughed softly, "You shameless woman, you do have some sense of modesty." His teasing murmur carried no farther than her hearing.

"Sorry," Tom apologized after averting the flashlight. "Do you want to return the call a little later?"

"No. I'll take it." Turning again to Deborah, he ordered quietly, "You wait here a minute."

With effortless strokes, he swam to the edge of the pool. Shaking the hair out of his face, he levered himself out of the water onto the cement deck. His clean, male lines sent Deborah's heart thudding against her ribs as he walked to the shed where they had left their clothes. From inside, he pulled out a long beach towel and began wiping himself dry.

"You'd better go tell them I'll be there in a minute, Tom," he instructed, stepping into his trousers.

"Right away." The flashlight was turned toward the house, its light outlining Tom's silhouette as he started across the courtyard. His footsteps made no sound in the snow, but the light kept getting smaller until it disappeared in the thickening snowfall. By the time the sound of a door closing echoed into the night, Zane had pulled his sweater on and was walking to the side of the pool, carrying the large beach towel.

"You can come out now." He waited at the ladder and Deborah swam to it.

Her toe touched the bottom rung when she remembered. "What about my bathing suit?"

There was a wicked glint in his blue eyes as he slanted her a smile. "It's too dark to find it now. We'll just have to wait until morning." He shook out the towel. "Come on. It's getting cold out here."

Grabbing hold of the ladder rail, Deborah climbed out of the pool. Immediately, the chill of the air's low temperature shivered over her bare flesh, the evaporating pool water cooling her skin even more. Before she could reach for the towel, Zane was swinging it behind her and wrapping it around her shoulders. When he started to overlap the towel in front, his hands paused in their task. His gaze roamed up her leggy length to linger on the rise and fall of her breasts, firm and creamy smooth. Deborah trembled as much from the desire in his look as from the cold. At last his gaze trailed the last distance to her warm gray eyes.

"God, you're beautiful, Deborah," Zane declared with a strangled groan and tightly overlapped the beach towel to enclose her in a cocoon.

She gave a little cry of surprise as he unexpectedly picked her up and carried her to the shed. Without putting her down, he somehow managed to reach inside and retrieve her shoes and robe, adding them to his burden. Then he started for the house.

"What are you doing?" Deborah protested.

"I don't have the control to stand by and watch you dress. And I'm not leaving you out here so you can fall and crack your head," he told her flatly. His mocking blue eyes challenged her to argue with him. He wouldn't listen to words and the towel was virtually a straight jacket. Also, they were already halfway across the courtyard. "Besides you are cold." Zane voiced the last factor that had kept her silent. "There isn't any point wasting time getting dressed when I can have you inside where it's warm."

"You've thought of everything," she said, trying to keep her teeth from clattering together.

He suddenly looked away, his expression turning grim. "Not everything." Deborah knew without asking that he was talking about their future and its uncertain course.

Entering the house through the rear door, Zane carried her all the way into her bedroom before setting her down. His hands gripped the sides of her arms, not allowing the towel to loosen. The brevity of his kiss was hard with regret.

"Go take a hot shower and get to bed," he told her and started to leave.

"Zane." Deborah abandoned her pride to ask, "Are you coming back?"

"No." He looked at her, noting the towel that had slipped off one shivering shoulder. "Not tonight. And not because it isn't what I'd like to do." He bent and kissed her ivory shoulder before covering it with the towel.

"Then why?" She tried to sound casually interested and not as lonely as she felt.

"Maybe it's too late, but I have to consider the consequences of our actions—for your sake as well as my own." His hand stroked her cheek in a farewell caress as Deborah accepted his answer with a stoic calm.

Then he was striding out of her room. Deborah refused to accept the possibility that she might lose him, that she might have enjoyed a brief glimpse of happiness. After showering and slipping into her nightclothes, she went to bed and dreamed about Zane and falling snow.

THE NEXT MORNING, Deborah had dressed and was about to leave her bedroom for the breakfast table when there was a knock at her door. Her heart gave a leap of excitement at the thought that it might be Zane and she rushed the last few steps to the door. Madelaine was in the hallway. There was a bright twinkle in her brown eyes.

"I think this is yours." She handed Deborah a wet bundle.

A scarlet heat warmed her face as she recognized her swimsuit. "Yes, it is," she admitted with a self-conscious laugh.

"Obviously Zane took you swimming last night." Then Madelaine could contain herself no longer and gave Deborah a quick smile. "Don't look so embarrassed. I'm a nurse, remember. Besides, I know you are going to make Zane very happy."

"If he'll let me," Deborah murmured and walked to the bathroom to hang the wet suit over the tub.

"He should have his head examined if he doesn't," the brunette retorted.

"Is breakfast ready yet?" Deborah changed the subject.

"Jessie was just setting the table. Sylvia's tray is ready so I'm going to take it up to her room before the food gets cold. I'll see you at the table," Madelaine waved as she walked out. "And keep your chin up. Zane knows a good thing when he sees it."

Deborah smiled faintly and dried her hands on a towel before leaving the bedroom for the sun-brightened morning room where the breakfast was served. Zane was standing at a window when she entered the room. Deborah paused, feeling her pulse accelerate at the sight of his leanly muscled figure. If that mask of his shut her out again, she knew she would scream.

"Good morning." Her greeting was a deliberate attempt to draw his gaze.

He half turned to look at her. "Good morning." And there was no mask to conceal the warm light in his eyes. "I was just looking at the snow."

The world was white outside the window, but it

wasn't the morning that Deborah was thinking about. It was last night. The same memory was reflected in his glittering look.

"It's beautiful, isn't it?" she said.

Zane crossed the room to stand in front of her. His hand shaped itself to the side of her neck while his thumb drew lazy circles under her chin. It was a seductive caress to which she was all too susceptible.

"Breakfast is ready. And we have a lot of work to do today, Miss Holland." The glinting light in his eyes mocked his own formality. Then his mouth was moving over her lips with a sweet, drugging force that ended just as Deborah was becoming hopelessly addicted to its influence. He took her hand and led her to the table, seating her in a chair next to his.

Work was exactly what he had in mind, but it was conducted with a difference. Zane kept finding excuses to touch her—a hand caressing her shoulder or resting on the back of her waist while he studied the notes she was making. He smiled a lot, almost every time he looked at her. The obvious change in his behavior was noted by Tom.

"Swimming at night seems to improve your disposition, Zane," he remarked at one point. "You should do it more often." His gentle glance encompassed Deborah, signaling his approval of a relationship he had once counseled against.

At five o'clock, Zane glanced at his watch. "We'll quit for today." He began stacking the papers in front of him.

"Why so early?" Deborah frowned. Ever since the office had been transferred to the house, they had worked at least an hour longer.

"Have you forgotten? We're having a dinner party tonight. I thought you would want time to get ready."

She had forgotten. Too much had happened since Madelaine had volunteered her as hostess. She uttered her first thought, "What should I wear?"

"Don't tell me you don't have anything to wear?" Zane mocked. "I bought you a closetful of dresses."

His reminder sidetracked her. "Why did you buy me those gowns? Were you ashamed of what I wore?" She remembered how her pride had been bruised by that incident.

"You would be stunning in anything. I think I just delighted in showing you off," he shrugged.

"That's a diplomatic answer," Deborah responded with a trace of irritation and disappointment. "No wonder you are such a successful businessman."

Zane studied her for a long moment. "All right. The truth is I was defensive about you even then. I didn't want some snob like Foster Darrow's wife or daughter making disparaging remarks about your clothes. I knew we'd be seeing a lot of them during the negotiations. I didn't want them to hurt you," he finished on a taut note, then flashed her a smile. "Now, go make yourself more beautiful."

CHAPTER ELEVEN

SINCE THE PARTY was a pre-Christmas celebration, Deborah chose a velvet dress of kelly green. The silver filigree brooch was her grandmother's, a lovely piece of costume jewelry but with little antique value. She wore her auburn hair loose, the way Zane liked it, and silver hoops in her ears.

There were butterflies in her stomach as she walked to the living room. The invited guests were Zane's friends. It was important that they like her, important to her if no one else. She tried to calm her jittery nerves with a deep breath. Inside the living room, she stopped as Zane swept her with a slow glance.

"How do I look?" Her self-confidence was decidedly lacking at this moment.

"Like a Christmas tree." His crooked smile was lightly teasing. He moved leisurely across the room to let his hand finger a russet curl. "You are beautiful, Deborah."

The doorbell rang and the guests began arriving. Zane smoothly explained that his wife was not feeling well and everyone seemed to tacitly understand what he had left unsaid. Deborah was introduced as his assistant. No one questioned her position but she received a few curious glances, and speculating looks were exchanged between couples. Yet she wasn't made to feel uncomfortable—not by them.

With each passing hour, Zane had become more and more aloof, speaking less, avoiding her eyes whenever she looked at him, and donning that mask again. Deborah had the impression that she was somehow to blame. As the evening dragged on, she had to force the smile that curved her mouth and the responses to the small talk of the guests. When the front door closed on the last guest, her nerves were stretched as taut as piano wire.

The silence in the house was deafening as Zane walked past her to return to the living room. Deborah followed him, confused and angry. After unplugging the tree lights, he walked to the fireplace and stirred the dying embers. A shower of sparks cascaded into the gray ashes. Deborah watched the silent death of the fire and knew she wasn't going to let hers end that way.

"What is it, Zane? What have I done wrong?" she demanded.

His back remained to her. He continued to stare at the banked fire, demonstrating impatience in the way he gripped the fireplace poker. "Nothing. You belonged tonight, Deborah." His voice seemed to come from some deep, dark place. "It felt right to have you by my side greeting the guests, right to have you sitting at the opposite end of the table from me, and right to walk our guests to the door. I wanted to choke every time I had to call you my assistant." He spun angrily. "But what else could I call you with my wife upstairs?"

"I am your assistant. . . unless you fired me in the

last six hours," Deborah pointed out in a tremor of relief.

"You know what I mean." He jammed the poker in its stand, metal clanging with the force of his anger.

"Yes, I do." It was a consolation to her pride that Zane was bothered by her position. She moved slowly across the room to the fireplace and lifted her face to his. "But I've accepted it."

"Well, dammit! I won't!" he exploded.

"What else can you do?" she reasoned quietly.

His eyes blazed over her face. With a groan, he gathered her into his arms and crushed her lips beneath his. It was a wild, desperate need that tore at her heart. The raw emotion of his kiss enveloped her, making her weak because it echoed her feelings.

From another part of the house came a startled outcry, followed by a loud thumping. They broke apart, both looking toward the open doorway to the hall. Deborah cast a frowning glance toward Zane.

"What was that?"

"I don't know." His jaw tightened in ominous grimness. He set Deborah away from him and started for the door.

Deborah hesitated only a second before she followed him, hurrying to keep up with his long strides. More sounds could be heard coming from the staircase...and voices...Madelaine's voice, then Frank's. The staircase was enclosed, except for the last short flight. As Deborah rounded the hall corner behind Zane, she saw Madelaine crouched beside a still figure on the landing. Sylvia Wilding had fallen down the steps. Zane rushed up the short flight to his wife's side.

"What happened?" He shot the question at Madelaine.

"I thought she was asleep and I stepped out of the room just for a moment. She slipped out while I was gone. Frank is calling an ambulance." She smoothed blond hair away from the forehead of the unconscious woman.

Zane bent over her, then shook his head in tired anger. "She's drunk."

"I know. I found a third of a bottle of rum in her room," Madelaine admitted. "It's probably what Jessie had left over from the eggnog."

"Why didn't she lock it up?" he demanded harshly.

"For all we know, Sylvia might have a key to the cabinet." Madelaine straightened from her patient to glare at him. "Why don't you give up, Zane? You simply can't keep her here. You want her to have her own room, be free to come and go as she pleases, and not be locked in. You want her to live in a normal atmosphere, but Sylvia is not normal! She needs constant care and supervision. I can't give it to her. This isn't a controlled environment. Give up, Zane. She doesn't belong here."

There was a clatter of footsteps on the stairs and Frank came into view at the landing. "The ambulance is on its way."

"Is it necessary?" Zane questioned, without anger this time.

"I think she might have a concussion, maybe a cracked rib." The brunette nurse had regained her professional poise. "I'd rather be safe and have an ambulance take her to the hospital than drive her there ourselves."

By the time the wail of the ambulance sirens entered the driveway, Tom and Jessie had joined Deborah at the base of the stairs. As the attendants lifted Sylvia Wilding onto the stretcher, Zane glanced at Deborah.

"I'm going to the hospital with her," he said.

"Of course," she nodded.

"I'll come with you," Tom volunteered.

Zane hesitated, then nodded his agreement. Seconds later, Sylvia was being wheeled out by the attendants. Madelaine went along, too, but Frank stayed behind. The sirens wailed again as the ambulance drove away.

Deborah waited up until after midnight before she finally gave up the vigil and went to bed. Tom was at the breakfast table the next morning when she entered.

"Good morning. How is Sylvia?" she asked.

"A slight concussion and a lot of bruises. Other than that, she wasn't hurt. It's a miracle, but I guess it was because she was drunk," he shrugged.

"It must have been late when you came back. I suppose Zane is still sleeping," Deborah guessed.

"He didn't come back with us."

"He stayed at the hospital with Sylvia?" Something in his tone made her phrase the sentence as a question.

"No."

"Where did he go?"

"I don't know." Tom shook his head and spread more jam on his toast.

"Surely you must have some idea," she insisted.

"I have some, yes, but I'm not going to guess

where he is or what he's doing," he answered. "I deal in facts and statistics."

"Did...did he say when he'd be back?"

"No."

Without Zane to add to her workload, Deborah finished the backlog of papers, memos, and reports that had accumulated on her desk. It helped the day pass, but the evening dragged. No one was willing to venture an opinion of where Zane might be. Since no one else seemed to be worried, Deborah tried not to be either.

Zane wasn't at the breakfast table the next morning. She refused the pancakes and sausages Jessie brought and settled for juice and coffee instead. The others were still at the table eating when Deborah left to go to the study.

The doors were ajar. Deborah hesitated outside because they were always kept closed. She hurried inside to find Zane standing at a window looking out. He glanced over his shoulder when she entered, then turned back.

"Welcome back." The words came out in an eager rush. "Where have you been?"

"I've arranged to have Sylvia committed. She'll have twenty-four-hour, professional care, the best in the country." Zane continued to stare out the window.

"I'm sorry."

"The doctors aren't sure that she will ever get better. Whatever I felt for her, died a long time ago. Our marriage has just been some words on a piece of paper for years now."

"It was a difficult decision for you." Deborah

wanted to get close to him, but his attitude was keeping her at a distance, almost physically holding her away.

"Yesterday afternoon I had my attorney file for a divorce." Zane turned to look at her after he had issued the statement. "There isn't any doubt that I'll get a decree, but there's something you have to know. My marriage to Sylvia was dead long before you came on the scene; this decision would have been made anyway, whether or not I had ever met you. Her love for me was as dead as mine for her. But circumstances being what they are, I can never entirely walk out on her, or shelve my responsibility toward her. Even when you are my wife, Deborah, in one respect Sylvia's needs must always come first.

"It may not sound fair, but I *am* responsible for her—there's no one else who cares about her. She needs me and I have to be there when she does. She was the mother of my son, and I can't just abandon her."

A tremulous smile curved Deborah's lips. "You wouldn't be the man I love if you could, Zane."

Her response eliminated the icy mask forever. Zane started toward her and she met him halfway. Outside, the sun glistened on pure white drifts of snow.

Where passion and destiny meet...
there is love

Jesse's Lady

Veronica Sattler

Brianna Deveraux had a feisty spirit matched by that of only one man, Jesse Randall. In North Carolina, 1792, they dared to forge a love as vibrant and alive as life in their bold new land.

Harlequin Intrigue

Because romance can be quite an adventure.